MASTER ME

A DARK MAFIA ROMANCE

MASTERS OF CORISICA

JANE HENRY

J HENRY PUBLISHING INC.

Copyright © 2023 by Jane Henry

All rights reserved.

No part of this book may be reproduced in any form or by any electronic or mechanical means, including information storage and retrieval systems, without written permission from the author, except for the use of brief quotations in a book review.

Cover art by Jason O'Bannon

SYNOPSIS

Savannah is beautiful. Brilliant. Brighter than a ray of sunshine.

She's also way too young for me and practically family.

But she's in trouble.

When she witnesses a murder at the hands of rival mafia, Savannah flees to the only safe refuge she knows — my family.

My life is ordered. Careful. Disciplined. But when Savannah needs protection, I can't turn her away.

I offer her a deal: I'll take her into my custody. Hide her in plain sight at Le Luxe, the club I own and operate for those who understand the pleasure that comes with total surrender.

I'll keep her safe, no matter the cost.

In return, she'll follow my rules. Masquerade as the perfect submissive.

Obey me.

Our ruse might save her life...but will it save her from me?

ONE

Savannah

Paris.

Is.

Awesome.

I draw in a deep breath, close my eyes, and release it. The warm rays of the setting sun kiss my skin like a blessing, and I am here for it.

"Nicolette, I swear, the Parisian air smells different. It's just so... cleansing." It helps that we're eating dessert in one of Paris's finer restaurants, bathed in the scent of cheese and wine. One of the cool things about Parisians is that they eat cheese literally any time of day, but most especially as a little palate cleanser between dinner and dessert. On the table in front of me sits a half-eaten plate of crème brûlée, a dessert that's as fun to eat as it is to say.

"It's not exactly fragrant in the metro," Fabien mutters with a grimace. True, true.

Nicolette smiles at me and winks.

Her husband can be grouchy, but he's good to her, and that's all that matters. Hell, I think the whole grouchiness thing runs in the family, because his brother Thayer's not exactly a ray of sunshine.

With him it's somehow... *hot,* though. All that brooding male power and testosterone. He oozes power with those corded, finely honed muscles, and that firm jawline I want to lick—

I catch that stray thought before it gets me into some serious Parisian trouble.

I decide I don't care, not about grouchiness or what it would take to soothe that line on Thayer's brow, or anything that might tamper with my current state of mind, because Nicolette and I are seriously living the life. The French are responsible for the phrase *laissez-faire* after all.

We live in Paris now. Thanks to my sister we've got more money in our bank account than I ever thought possible, and I'm in grad school.

What could go wrong?

"Savannah," Nicolette says in that big sister tone I've learned to dread.

"Mmm?"

"We have to talk."

Uh oh.

I try to avert the crisis of a serious conversation. I lean back and close my eyes, basking in the setting rays of the sun. "Girl, do not harsh my mellow."

My sister raises an eyebrow. "Don't harsh your what?"

"My mellow, babe. I am loving life, and I am not in the mood for a lecture."

"When are you ever in the mood for a lecture?"

I open one eye to look at Nicolette, whose own eyes are twinkling at me. She reaches over and tugs my hair, just like she used to when we were little, and smiles. Ever since our parents died, Nicolette's matured, and she takes her job as big sister pretty seriously. "I wasn't gonna lecture you. I just want to... talk."

I stifle a groan. I'm not sure there's much of a distinction between lecture and talk, but okay.

I know Nicolette's concerned for me. I know she worked her ass off to earn the money we have, and though I don't know the intricacies of it all, I suspect it had something to do with Fabien's business in Paris and south of here in Corsica.

What he does isn't exactly legal, but sometimes ignorance is bliss. Since I like bliss, I've chosen ignorance.

"Alright, then," I say, steeling myself. I sit up straighter and give Nicolette my undivided attention. I fold my hands in front of me. "What shall we discuss?"

I shoot a quick glance at Fabien, hoping he's busy on his phone or something. He's more of the lecture type, and his input will definitely change the course of this conversation. No such luck.

Fabien clears his throat. My brother-in-law's the eldest in his family. With two younger brothers of his own, he's easily adopted the role of big brother to me, overprotection free of charge. So I have a tendency to sort of wilt a little under his serious look. The Gerard family is well-respected—dare I say, even feared—in France, and there's good reason.

Like his brothers, Fabien is huge and muscled, filthy rich, and hot as hell. My sister scored the whole damn package. But the point is, people pay attention to the Gerards.

Fabien speaks bluntly. "You need a bodyguard."

Oh no. Not this again. I snort. "Bodyguard? Do we really need to come back to that?" I shake my head. I lower my voice, so we don't draw attention.

I am pretty convinced that having a bodyguard for protection isn't a normal thing. And even though I am all about the shopping, the super swanky little flat, and going to grad school debt free, I draw a line at the whole bodyguard thing.

"You guys," I say, less resistant this time. "I really do appreciate your concern. You know I do. But I'm a grad student. I'm super careful. I'm not a party animal, and I'm rarely even out past dark. It's just overkill, you guys."

Both of them stare at me, unmoved. Nicolette sighs.

My sister, as beautiful and put-together as always, looks a bit older when her brow knits in concern.

"It's not overkill, Savannah," she says in a low voice. "Trust me on this one. Why do you object to this so much?"

I try an angle she might understand. "Because I am hardly a celebrity. And bodyguards are, like, for celebrities and important people. I'm just not that special, and don't give me that 'oh you *are* special' lecture again. You might as well give me a participation trophy."

Nicolette's lips press in a thin line. "You just don't want someone following you."

I cannot pull the wool over my big sister's eyes.

"Well, yeah," I say, still trying to plead my case. The truth is, though, that even though I'm an adult, and a competent one at that, my sister is fully responsible for paying my bills. She wants to, and it's important to her. Plus, I'm flat-out broke, so I wasn't foolish enough to decline what she offered.

That puts me a bit at her mercy, though. While she's no longer my legal guardian, I am sort of her responsibility.

Nicolette shoots a quick glance toward Fabien. I quake a little at the look on his face, as he's grown a little more serious. A bit more stern.

"We can't make you have a guard if you don't want one," he says, with a tightening of his jaw that sort of implies he wishes he could. "We aren't your legal guardians, and you are an adult. We can, however, make strong recommendations that are in your favor."

He doesn't usually lecture *me*, but he's damn intimidating. And even though he's only ever been good to me, I know he's capable of... shall we say... scary things.

I know he wouldn't hurt me.

Would he?

Before I came here and met him, I warned Nicolette. I told her that the Gerard family was known for being a new but tenacious organized crime ring. I wouldn't have known a thing if Fabien's friend hadn't sort of tipped me off.

Last year, Fabien sent one of his friends from Boston to provide security for me.

When I found out Fabien's friend's name was Mario Rossi, I put two and two together. Everyone in Boston knows the Rossi family name: known mafia, feared, powerful... and friends with the Gerard family. I'm not exactly an expert on the mafia, but I do know that being friends with a known mob is a pretty decent red flag.

So I took a risk one night and casually mentioned something about the Gerard family to Mario, implying I knew full well they were mafia.

Mario went right along with it. "Not as large as we are," he said. "They're newer, but rapidly growing."

I had my answer.

So even though Fabien has never given me reason to fear him, at the back of my mind, I know what he's capable of. The knowledge makes me a bit more guarded. I'm on my best behavior around him. I'm... kinda not sure what he'd do if I wasn't.

Fabien glances at his phone. "Dammit. We need to go. We were supposed to leave for the airport ten minutes ago." The two of them are on their way to Italy.

I wave my hand at the table. "I'll get this," I say, flashing my sister a magnanimous grin.

Standing, she winks at me. "Don't think this conversation is over."

I roll my eyes and stand, giving them both Parisian air kisses on the cheek.

"Savannah," Fabien says. "We won't be reachable for at least the next two hours."

I can tell he's not a fan of this scenario. Typically, even when flying they have their private jets or planes with internet access so we aren't out of touch, but they had to book a separate flight this time on a commercial plane. Even though they fly business class, their flight isn't internet-equipped.

"Gotcha." I'm already sitting back down and taking out my wallet.

"Which is exactly why I wish she had a guard," Nicolette says in a low voice to Fabien.

Fabien nods. Honestly, I wouldn't put it past him to assign a guard to me just for the hell of it, without telling me or even his wife. Their family home, which is also their primary headquarters, isn't far from here.

"If you need anything at all, Thayer's flown in from Corsica this weekend, and you know where to reach him."

I try to focus on what Fabien's telling me, but when he mentions his brother's name, my mind sort of short-circuits.

I'd hoped he'd be in Corsica, since they have all sorts of businesses and connections there. It's easy to pretend to forget about someone when they're on an island, and not in the city where you actually live.

Le Sauvage, they call him. The Savage.

I don't know how he earned that name, but a part of me wants to know.

I would absolutely die before I'd admit it to anyone, but I have a relentless, uncontrollable, schoolgirl crush on Thayer.

Why me?

Why him?

He is the grumpiest asshole in the family.

Every scowl he sends my way makes my heart turn in my chest.

Wait, what were we talking about?

Thayer.

In case of emergency.

Got it.

"Perfect. Listen," I tell Nicolette. "When I was in America, I didn't have a guard, and I was fine. I'm not sure what's changed. If anything, I'm closer to you now than before."

I don't meet her eyes. My sister can see right through me, and I'll bet Fabien can, too, which is almost worse, because the man has the power to literally wilt me with a stare.

"The difference is you're in Paris now," Fabien says as he holds Nicolette's jacket up for her to slide into. I'm surprised to find my eyes misting with tears.

I want that.

I want someone to care about me the way Fabien cares about Nicolette. He might be a criminal, but the man knows how to take care of a woman. The gentleman mob boss, if ever there was one.

I swallow the knot in my throat that threatens to choke me and signal to the waitress.

"We'll talk about this when we get back," Nicolette says in such a tone I'm surprised she didn't add *young lady* to the end. She reaches for my hand and squeezes it.

"Alright," I agree. "You kids have fun in Italy. I can't wait to hear all about it, and don't forget to bring me back something!" I've never outgrown my childish need for souvenirs.

"Of course not," Nicolette says with a wink. "Love you!"

The lump grows again. "I love you, too," I say with a sigh.

I sit at the table after they're gone.

I eat the last of the crême brûlée and sip the last of the wine. I watch the sun sink beneath the roof of the restaurant.

When I stand and finally stretch my limbs, evening has fully descended.

The streets of Paris are typically well lit, but like most old European cities, some sections still hearken to days gone by—brick buildings, cobblestoned streets, streetlamps that have stood for decades.

God, I love Paris. If I could marry Paris, we'd elope.

The tourist guides all say that Paris is safe for a single woman. Even the Eiffel Tower's structure has been outfitted with hundreds of yellowish spotlights that not only highlight the landmark, but also provide visibility and safety for nighttime visitors. Here in France, we have trains and buses and rental cars at the ready, and policemen aren't far away if we need them.

I'm safe, I tell myself as I step outside the restaurant and into the cooler evening air. Across the street, a rowdy crowd of young adults chats and laughs, one gesturing wildly as if he's telling a story. A pang hits me in the chest.

Heh. I must be hormonal. I'm not usually this emotional all over the place like this. What's going on with me?

Am I... lonely?

Me, world traveler and student—*correction*, wealthy world traveler and grad student—who lives in the swankiest apartment and eats the best food and wears truly fabulous clothes... is lacking in something?

Maybe rumors float through school about my affiliation with the Gerards. Maybe Parisians are just a close-knit sort of people that don't easily take on new friendships. Or maybe I just haven't given it enough time, but I'm... well, sort of friendless here.

I shove my hands in my pockets and decide to walk instead of taking a cab. It's a lovely night, and there are lots of people out here... and my overprotective sister and brother-in-law are on a flight to Italy and can't stop me.

The sound of my footsteps on the hard sidewalk click clacks down the streets as I leave behind the noise of the city and walk toward our little apartment. One of the reasons we got such a deal on this place was that it's a good walk from our apartment to the other parts of the city where we find restaurants and shopping venues.

I pull out my phone on instinct and check the texts.

Nicolette:

> Hey. Be safe, please. I know you're not a kid but you're my sister and the only one I've got!!

Cue a whole string of heart emojis.

Me:

> I promise, I will not drink more than ten drinks at a time, will only smoke high-end pot, and have casual sex ONLY every other day, m'kay?

I can almost hear her sighing on the other end of the phone.

Nicolette:

> Alright, sounds good. Love you, you big goof.

I smile and text her back.

Me:

> Love you, too

I continue to walk, my head down, when a surprising brisk gust of air makes me shiver. I pull my jacket tighter around me and come to a sudden stop.

Wait.

There's got to be some kind of a carnival or something happening this weekend, because the street looks different.

This is... unusual. Stalls are set up in various places, changing the appearance of landmarks. I'm all turned around. I look about me, trying to locate something I recognize, when I realize with a sinking feeling in the pit of my stomach...

I don't know where I am.

My heart gives a little thump when I try to get a good idea of my location. I have to admit. This might've been a good time for me to... alright, fine, have a guard. Someone I could at least wave to and ask for a little directional help?

I glance back at my phone and notice it's almost dead.

I stifle a groan. Nicolette would have my head.

I look around again. Maybe there's someone nearby that can tell me where to go. A pub or a little corner store or a friendly old lady? But I walked myself right out of anything familiar or populated.

Well.

I'll just have to go back the way I came.

I might be alone, but I'm safe.

I turn around and walk back in the general direction of where I started, but when I come to an intersection, I wonder. Is it left or straight?

Left. It has to be left. I think I remember that little house with the sign for the flats for rent.

I walk faster now. I'm dying to get home to our flat where my books wait. The newest Ilona Andrews book just came in the mail, and I can't wait to dig in.

A feeling of dread grows in my belly as I don't recognize anything nearby.

Where... am I?

None of this is familiar.

I've never seen this house. I've never seen this street. I don't recognize the street names, and now that the sun's set, I don't even know what general direction I'm walking in.

Ahead of me, I hear voices and stifle a dry sob that surprises even myself. I didn't know I was that wound up.

When I turn a corner, I almost cry in relief when I see the brilliant, welcoming glow of a streetlight in front of a pub, the door wide open, and about half a dozen men talking amongst themselves. When they see me, they stop talking for a minute.

I don't usually have regrets. But right now? I am so regretting dying my hair highlighter pink. I stand out like a flag on a wide-open field.

Maybe I should've listened to my sister, who would've wanted to shake me for walking alone, at night, in Paris, which the tour guides might say is safe but it's still a large, bustling city.

One of the men staring at me gives me a lewd grin that makes the little hairs on my neck stand up. Ugh. I can imagine Fabien's reaction. Funny how a few minutes ago I was eager for more independence, but right about now I'd give anything for my brother-in-law's imposing presence and my sister's fearlessness.

"Salut! C'est une très belle tenue que vous portez."

Oh, how cliché to compliment me on my outfit.

But no, I am not playing this game.

So I do what any intelligent, self-aware woman would do in this situation. I smile and lie and pretend I don't speak his language.

"Pardon. Je ne parle pas français."

I walk past them and turn a corner. I'm holding my breath.

But no one follows me.

Oh, thank God.

I breathe out in relief, only to find myself at the back of the pub. Trash barrels and empty boxes line the walls, and the air reeks of something I can't identify and don't want to. I wonder if I should go inside and try to find a phone, when I realize with a jolt of alarm... I'm not alone.

Fear knots in my stomach at the chilling scene in front of me. A woman, gagged and bound, in the hands of two big, terrifying, fully armed men. I stand motionless in horror at the sight.

At the pleading look in her eyes, panic explodes within me. She screams and begs against the gag, but only garbled sounds come out.

No.

I open my mouth to speak. To tell them to let her go, to do something, when one curses and the second turns his weapon toward me.

"Get out of here," he snaps at me in French. "Get the fuck out."

I can't move. I open my mouth to speak, but I'm staring down the barrel of a pistol.

Let her go, I scream in my head. *Let her go!*

But I can't talk.

"You have three seconds," he growls. I don't know what to do. I feel as if I've been frozen into ice by a magic wand. I hear the click of his gun.

I'm going to die. I'm not going to save her, and I'm going to die, right along with her.

I wish I'd told Nicolette I loved her before she left. Why didn't I tell her I loved her?

"Drop your weapon!"

They're looking over my shoulder. I'm afraid to even turn around.

My heart beats so fast I feel dizzy. I stifle a whimper.

The problem is, neither of the armed men make a move to drop their weapon. The woman begins to sob and shake as a uniformed officer, dressed in the trademark dark blue of *la Police Nationale*, steps around me with his weapon drawn.

It happens so fast I don't have time to blink.

One of the men curses. The other pulls the trigger. The woman screams against her gag as the officer crumples to the ground.

My intuition screams at me.

Run.

A bullet pings and ricochets off a metal dumpster as I run as far away from here as I can get.

"Go get her!" one of the men shouts to the other. "Kill her!"

I have to think fast. He'll expect me to keep running until he catches me. I'm faster than the lumbering idiot chasing me, so when I turn a corner, I'm out of his line of sight. I duck down a narrow passageway and into a doorway. I flatten myself against the door, completely covered in shadow. I hold my breath while he races past me. I wait until I hear no more footsteps.

Then I wait some more.

I stand in place until the night becomes an inky blanket of black velvet and my feet fall asleep.

My phone is dead. I have no idea where I am.

And I've just witnessed a murder.

I wish I could call my sister.

I want to cry.

TWO

*T*HAYER

"Thayer, you here?" Lyam yells.

I stretch and stand, my muscles aching from sitting too damn long at the desk. I shut off my computer, put the pens back in the penholder, and straighten the calendar.

Fabien says I have a hair across my ass. Asshole.

My mother calls my tendencies "quirks." I call them habits. I like my shit clean.

"In the office," I yell back.

Footsteps approach seconds before there's a rapid knock on the door.

"Come in."

Lyam opens the door and enters with our friend, Mario Rossi. Youngest brother of the Rossi family in America, we became friends a few years ago over a trade our brothers initiated. We agreed it would be useful having mutual friends overseas, for both of us, and we weren't wrong.

"Rossi," I say warmly, extending my hand to shake his. "Didn't expect you tonight."

"Yeah, I wasn't supposed to be in until next week, but duty called, and Romeo sent me out early. Grabbed the first flight out."

The Rossi family has business in Tuscany, a short flight from here, and since we formed an alliance, they've begun to do business in Paris as well.

"You know you're welcome here anytime."

"You know why he's here. Who wants a hotel when you can eat at Chez Gerard?"

The Rossis are sort of famous for their bottomless appetites and love of good food.

Mario playfully punches his arm, and Lyam dodges a second jab.

"I won't lie," Mario begins. "It's true. So have you taken over here since Fabien tied the knot?"

I shake my head and walk toward the exit. "Not really. I was taking over business and surveillance before then. It's just better to have me here now that Fabien's traveling more." And going off the grid and spending time with his wife.

For days and full weekends at a time.

I lead them to the door so I can lock up.

"Makes sense."

"You want a drink?"

"You know it. Brought a case of wine from Tuscany to your mother."

"Alright, then not only are you welcome, you can move in," Lyam says.

The Rossi family wine from Tuscany is the best I've ever had.

I shut and lock the door to the office, one of the best rooms in this large, rambling house of ours. Though we each have residences in Corsica and privately, we always manage to meander back to our family home in Paris. Makes sense, though, since Paris is the hub for so much of the work we do.

"How's married life treating you?" Lyam asks.

Mario grins. "Gloria's amazing."

"Been a while now?"

"Few years, yeah." He chuckles. "You next, Thayer? I heard Fabien's a goner."

Me? Marriage?

"Oh hell, no."

There's a reason why every woman I've ever been with has been a member of Le Luxe. Le Luxe, the most exclusive club in Corsica—hell, the *only* master/slave club in Corsica, is my primary place of business, so I haven't taken a partner in a long time.

Women at the club don't require affection. They don't require aftercare, or coddling, or any of the other bullshit a real relationship requires.

They live to serve. They know their needs are met.

Good enough for me.

The house is quiet as we walk down the hall. The housekeepers and staff have either gone to bed or left for the day, and Maman goes to bed early, so it's just us here. It feels strange that Fabien isn't here like he used to be. Family dynamics always change when people get married, have children.

I'm not sure I like change. I like things predictable, neat, and ordered.

We head to the living room, where my father insisted we install a full bar. Lyam's been mixing drinks since he was twelve.

"What's your drink, Rossi?"

Mario grins. "When in Rome..."

Lyam fancies himself a mixologist, so he waves his magic wand and hands us both a few potent concoctions. I have no idea what they are, but I'm not complaining. I sigh after the first sip. I didn't know how badly I needed that.

"You know," Mario says almost casually, but I don't miss the sharp glint in his eyes. "In America, a married man is a made man."

"Same here," Lyam says. I glare at him but he's pouring a drink and misses it.

"Makes you more powerful. You get a wife and kids and you—"

"Might as well get shackles," I finish. Lyam laughs but Mario winces and shakes his head.

"I'm serious, Thayer. This outfit is new. Of the three of you, only one is married. You know if you marry a woman no one can touch her. You're a unit. Indivisible."

I try to divert the subject.

"You were always the player," I say. "You used to show up with a woman on each arm. What happened?"

The front door booms with a thudding, frantic flurry of knocks, followed by the doorbell ringing. I'm on my feet instantly, my heart racing. Another frenzied knocking follows the first. I hear my mother's bedroom door open and her rapid footfalls as she races to the landing. Tension mounts in the air, but I keep my head and check my weapon.

The last time we got hurried knocks this late at night, Fabien had been shot.

Something is wrong. Everyone knows who lives in this house, and no one, not even a well-meaning neighbor or salesperson, ever knocks on this door uninvited.

I get to the door first, Lyam and Maman right behind me. Mario stands behind us, his hand on his weapon. Lyam is armed as well.

I yank open the door and almost immediately fall backward when I'm tackled by a bundle of a woman. She grabs at me and hauls herself to standing. She's all tangled hair and torn clothing, but I know exactly who she is the second those mahogany eyes look into mine.

Normally artless and serene, as innocent as a dew-kissed flower at sunrise, she now looks at me with utter terror. Panic has swept the color from Savannah's face, and the grip on my arm's so tight it's painful.

I catch her before she falls.

I hold her.

No.

I fight the urge to push her behind me and race into the night, gun drawn, to bring justice to whoever chased her here. To kill whoever made her cry. But heroics and impulsivity don't mix, and it isn't the way I do things. So I draw in a breath and let it out slowly as I bring her into the house.

"Go," I snap at Lyam, who races in front of me with his gun drawn, calling on our guards.

As soon as she realizes she's clinging to me, she releases her hold as if touching me burns her hands. She blinks in the brightness of the overhead lights and wrings her hands.

"Thayer! Oh, God, Thayer!" She spares a second to look over her shoulder. "Shut the door!" she says with a strangled cry. "Lock the gates! Hurry!" I reach for the door to slam it as she does the same, making her clumsily fall against it. Lyam's out there, but he can handle himself.

Maman reaches us and gently takes her from me as I make the call.

"Close the gates. All circuits on standby. Weapons ready."

Mario steps in front of me as Lyam returns. "All clear for now but I've only checked the front gate. Come with me, Rossi?"

I shake my head. "Before anyone does anything, we need to find out what's going on. Then you two can go." With Fabien gone, I'm the one Lyam obeys and as our guest, Mario does the same. They wait, like leashed guard dogs frothing at the mouth. Lyam practically paws the ground in front of him.

I stand Savannah upright in front of me. "Tell me what happened. I want to know everything before they go out, so tell me why you're here."

She draws in a breath and speaks in a rush of words. "I saw a police officer murdered and the murderers are chasing me."

I feel my eyebrows rise. I jerk my chin to Mario and Lyam. "Go."

Maman covers her mouth with her hand as the door slams behind them.

I reach for Savannah's hand but pull back. I held her when she fell, but I won't let myself touch her. *I can't.*

She's the baby sister of my sister-in-law. We're practically related.

She's ten years younger than you.

"Let's go in the other room. I want to know everything. Every detail you can remember."

"She's hurt, Thayer," Maman says pleadingly, her arm around Savannah's shoulders. I look down at her torn clothing. Her knees are covered in gravel and blood. My anger becomes a blistering fury, clawing at me like a monster with talons and fangs.

I'll kill them.

I will find whoever scared her and threatened her and they will die a painful, torturous death.

I turn my fury on Savannah. "I thought you were with Fabien and Nicolette. Why are you alone? What happened?"

She flinches as if slapped, what little color that had been left on her face now gone. She blanches when she mumbles her reply on a half cry. "I saw someone murdered," she repeats in a choked voice. "I... I got lost. I was with them, yes, but they left on their flight to Italy, and I walked home."

She's making no sense. I can't shake the truth out of her. So I stifle a growl that will only scare her and nod, trying to stay calm.

"Go on."

"There was... a woman. She was all tied up and gagged and screaming."

"Where were you?"

"I—I don't know. I got lost. My phone was dead."

I grit my teeth. A lecture won't help right now.

"I was behind some kind of a pub. I saw them and they saw me. I didn't know what to do. An officer came and they—they killed him. Right there. I don't know what happened after that. I ran."

"Did they find you?"

"Not at first. Please, Thayer, lock your gates. I'm so afraid they were following me. I heard—I saw—I don't know what I saw. I hid for hours until I was so cold, and I thought they were gone. I remembered where you were near the Seine, so I made my way here, and I swear—I swear they followed me, Thayer."

She looks over her shoulder as if chased by a ghost and takes an involuntary step toward me.

I try to gentle my voice and fail. "If they followed you, they won't get you now."

Maman speaks up. She does what I wouldn't dare to do—runs a hand down the back of Savannah's wild hair and smoothes it down. "Hush, *mon amore*," she whispers. "Come tell us what happened, and we—" When she pauses, she corrects what she was about to say. "You're safe here. Believe me when I tell you, Thayer won't let anyone hurt you. Even if someone *did* manage to get past Lyam and Mario, no one will get past Thayer." She lowers her voice and swallows before she finishes. "And I do mean no one, love."

Savannah nods.

"Sit." I stifle the need to snap my fingers.

We're not in Le Luxe.

Savannah is not my slave.

Hell, she's not even my submissive.

Still, when she sits and lays her hands in her lap, she looks at me and my heart turns over in my chest.

I don't care that she's beautiful.

I don't care that she's dainty and graceful and everything I love in a woman.

I don't admire her perfect, shapely legs, or the way her lips part when she's afraid, or the long, sensitive fingers that graze her neck when she swallows...

Aw, hell.

I admire everything about her.

I don't remember staff coming in the room and handing me the first aid kit. I find it in my hands. Normally, in serious emergency situations like this I'd let staff handle it, but the thought of anyone but me touching her...

I can't touch her.

Before I know what's happening, I'm kneeling in front of Savannah.

"Thayer, allow me," Maman offers.

No.

"I've got it, Maman. Like you said, she's safe now. I'll make sure no one hurts her."

Ignoring my suggestion, Maman sits on the couch next to Savannah and reaches for her hand. "Can I get you anything?"

Savannah looks at Maman and her lower lip quivers. Maman reaches over to her and embraces her. She runs her hand down the length of Savannah's hair over and over until Savannah releases a shuddering sigh.

"Maman, why don't you have the staff prepare her a room?"

Maman lets her go. "I'll do that," she whispers to her. "Thayer, if you need anything at all, call me."

I nod as I open the first aid kit. My mind is reeling with the details she told me. If she was at Avelline's, this is a lot worse than she even knows. Last year, the Lyon family was arrested for a dual murder in the alley outside the restaurant. It was the first time we realized their enemies and ours frequented the establishment.

I'll ask her for more details, but right now, I tend to her wounds.

Maman leaves.

Mario and Lyam have yet to return.

Staff retreats when I give them a look that makes them scurry.

Savannah and I sit alone in the living room.

"Now tell me," I say, as I lift her leg to examine her injury. "Tell me everything you remember. Start from the beginning."

THREE

Savannah

Thayer Gerard is kneeling in front of me.

Touching me.

Sure, he's doctoring my wounds, and he's trying his best to take care of me, but I can't stop my mind from reeling.

Minutes ago, I came here gasping in fear. I was sure that the men who murdered that cop followed me. I snuck around the city trying to find something that would help me find my way here, to the only friends I have.

And now... the man who's the epicenter of every damn fantasy I've had in months is here.

Touching me.

Okay, so he's not exactly touching me in the way I've imagined, but right now, his hands—those strong, masculine, capable hands of his—are cradling my injured leg.

"How did you get this injury?"

"It's just a scrape," I tell him, trying to ignore the way I shake when he touches me. "I wouldn't exactly say it's an *injury*."

A sharp look makes me snap my mouth shut.

Okay, it's an injury.

"I fell when I was running," I tell him truthfully. Running for my *life,* convinced I was being followed, determined to survive.

"You ripped both knees and tore up your hands from one fall?"

I look down. For some reason, I'm ashamed, like I'm a clumsy child.

"It was... a few times," I say honestly. I look away. My cheeks heat with embarrassment.

"Savannah."

I've never heard his voice so gentle, yet he still holds the command of a man that's used to getting his way. I don't know what he does for work, but I would imagine it has literally nothing to do with doing what anyone else tells him to do.

"Yes?" I whisper.

He smells *so good*. All virile and masculine. I'm not sure if it's aftershave or bodywash or cologne, but I want to continue to sit here just so I can inhale deep lungfuls of him.

When he cradles my injured leg, he flicks away the fabric from the wound with his thumb. A thread gets caught in the torn shreds of my skin. I gasp and draw in a quick breath at the sudden sharp stab of pain.

"You've got bits of fabric embedded in the skin," he says with a scowl.

"I'm sorry," I say, though I'm not sure why.

He looks back up at me. "Savannah," he says sternly, that scowl between his brows making my heart go pitter-patter. There's my name again. My mind somehow short-circuits when he says my name.

Goddammit, I need to get a grip.

"Do not apologize. You were not the one who caused this." I have the strange and sudden desire to say *yes, sir*.

"You look angry."

Still holding my leg, his dark blue gaze meets mine. "I'm fucking furious, but not at you."

I nod and swallow, unsure of how to respond. I've never heard him string together so many words at once. He's a man of few words, dark and mysterious, and sometimes brooding.

We don't speak again while he treats my wounds.

I'm caught halfway between observing every detail of my interaction with Thayer—*he's touching me*—and reliving the shocking events of the night.

Someone's life was taken tonight. Someone who woke up this morning and likely ate breakfast with his family and fully anticipated coming home this evening, lies cold and lifeless. He was a man of the law. A uniformed officer. Someone who dedicated his life to justice, who provided safety to the vulnerable.

And now he's dead.

That quickly. One minute he was breathing, his heart beating, his body alive and vibrant. The next... he was gone.

I didn't even know him, yet I still feel a sudden rush of tears.

"Did that hurt?" Thayer's dark eyebrows knit in concern.

"Did what hurt?" I ask stupidly, my mind still turning over the details of a life taken so suddenly.

Thayer blinks. "The antiseptic." I look down to see my jeans damp with some kind of liquid he's clumsily poured over my wound. Nothing about Thayer is haphazard, so I'm surprised to see he spilled it at all. He's usually such a perfectionist.

"Here, let me. I can do it," I say, reaching for the cotton pad and small bottle of antiseptic. The slanting frown between his brows tells me *that's* not an option and he pauses only long enough to give me a cold, hard stare.

The collar of his shirt is open at the neck, revealing a hint of dark curls. I shiver and turn away, aware that I am having very inappropriate thoughts about a man who might as well be my *brother*.

My very much older brother, I remind myself.

But while he dabs the liquid on another clean cotton pad, I lean down to look at my injuries. He smells like fresh air, pine, and cedar with a little spice.

I realize he's talking to me.

"What?" I say, pretending that I'm not indulging in schoolgirl fantasies but maybe I'm a little traumatized.

I begin to shake when I remember what happened again. I close my eyes against a rush of anxiety that sends nausea swirling in my belly. I swallow and look at him.

"I said," he begins, holding my gaze for a little too long. I squirm. "It would be a lot easier to tend to these wounds if you removed your pants."

I blink as if I don't understand him.

"Is that the best pick-up line you could muster?"

I can't believe I just said that.

He narrows his eyes at me.

"Okay, so yeah, it probably would help, but I'm not crazy about... about removing my clothing," I say in a whisper. I look wildly around the room for something that will get me out of this situation, because I am so not taking off my pants in the middle of the Gerard family living room.

His eyes are trained on me, narrowed.

"Maybe we need to remove the bits of gravel embedded in your flesh," he chides. I wince at his scalding tone.

I nod.

Right.

Yes.

I should... remove my pants.

I reach for the button at my belly and flinch when I clench my hands. Good God, that hurts.

"Here," he says in a harsh whisper. "Let me."

And then his hands are on my waist and he's lifting me to stand.

"I'm going to hell for this," he says as he meets my eyes. "Just so we're clear."

"It's a strange, harsh world you live in that you think doctoring someone's wounds would send you to hell," I whisper.

But his hands are at my waist and he's expertly unfastening my pants.

Pushing them down my hips. Lowering them past my knees one by one, gently, making sure the fabric doesn't scrape against my wounds.

"That's not the part that would damn me," he says, shaking his head. "Now sit back down before I fucking do something I regret."

I'm standing in front of Thayer, who's kneeling in front of me. I'm in my panties. He's so close I can feel his warm breath on my skin. I imagine what it would be like if he held me.

This should... not be... erotic.

He's... doctoring me.

I was injured.

He's just being... *brotherly*.

"Are you laughing?" he asks, in that scowly-stern way that makes my heart flutter like butterfly wings.

"No," I lie, and totally bust out with another laugh. I'm choking on my attempt not to laugh and failing miserably. Oh, God, I have to stop laughing.

"Savannah." Thayer leans back on his haunches and fixes me with a harsh gaze with a hint of judgment behind it. He draws in a breath as if prepared to lecture me.

Mmm, lecture me, baby.

I'm giggling again, covering my mouth with my hand so he doesn't see, which is about the same thing as closing my eyes and hoping that means he doesn't see me.

Oh, God, I think the wildly swinging emotions of the night have me a little punchy.

"Yes?" I ask.

"What is so funny?"

"I—I don't want to tell you what's so funny."

It takes more courage than I think it would to say this, but I soldier on, because there's no way I'm telling him what's going on in my mind.

"You're damn lucky," he says under his breath.

I feel my cheeks suddenly flame. "Why is that?" My words sound choked.

He holds my gaze for a few disquieting seconds. I squirm.

"Nothing. It's nothing."

Wait, now that isn't fair.

"Okay, excuse me?" I ask. Nicolette says I have a temper and I should watch it, because one day it will get me in trouble. "You can't do that stopping in mid-sentence thing. You don't like when I do that, and yet you did the same thing!"

"It's called thinking before you speak, a concept I know is foreign to you."

Oh, what an ass! How could I have thought he was hot?

"Sometimes, the better choice is not to complete a thought out loud, or to keep one's thoughts to oneself."

"Oh, really, is that right, Mr. Smarty-pants?"

The Gerard boys speak fluent English, and my French is actually excellent, but I'm not sure the whole "Smarty-pants" thing translates well.

Thayer stands. I haven't forgotten that my pants are around my ankles.

I'm suddenly aware of every one of my senses, as if my simmering emotions have amplified them.

The feel of his hands on my skin. The way his breath burns me like I'm standing too close to a bonfire. His masculine scent, the deep vibration of his voice...

He reaches for my chin and holds it so I can't look away. Quaking under the look he's giving me, I stare at his lips, full and gently parted, like he wants to kiss me.

When he speaks, he bares his teeth to me like an animal. If I could step back, I would.

"Because if you were mine," he says in a low rumble that ignites every nerve in my body, "you wouldn't be allowed to hold things back from me. I'd train you to talk to me. To tell me what was on your mind and stop giving me bullshit answers and half-truths. You'd learn to speak honestly and answer my questions when I asked."

I stare, aghast. I'm not sure he's gotten the memo that this is the twenty-first century.

What's scarier is that I'm not sure I care. The latent threat in his words, delivered in that protective yet nearly overbearing tone, electrifies me.

"If you were mine," he continues, "I would discipline you for going out alone without a guard. You'd learn, and quickly, that putting yourself in danger merits swift and severe punishment."

I've forgotten that I'm standing in his living room in my panties. I've forgotten the stinging pain in my knees. I've forgotten my crush on him, how badly I wanted his attention, because now that I have it, I realize *He. Is. An. Asshole.*

"How dare you?" I hiss. "How *dare* you?"

"You asked," he retorts. "I responded."

"Then I guess I'm fucking lucky that I'm not yours, then," I seethe, even as I imagine myself sprawled over his lap while he punishes me. Even though a part of me craves the thought of belonging to him. Warring desire and shock make my body tremble at the thought of him taking me across his knee. Tied to his bedpost so he can... discipline me.

What other dark and devious things would he do to me?

I want to know.

Oh. My. God.

I can't deny that the thought both horrifies and excites me.

Is that what being with a man like Thayer means?

How could I ever have a crush on someone like him?

I'm turning away when the sudden memory of what I saw tonight overcomes me. That woman tied up and terrified, dragged between two men like she was nothing but chattel...

I look back to him.

We're too close.

Too close.

"Are you sure about that, love?"

He's breathing heavily as his fingers skate up the length of my arm, wrapping me in a cocoon of heavy, heated anticipation. The touch of his hand sends shockwaves through my body, and when he cups my jaw, my heart threatens to leap out of my chest. Thayer's sharp blue eyes hold mine. My body vibrates with tension.

No, of course I'm not sure about that. I'm not sure at all.

His mouth hovers over mine. Part of me yearns to submit to this, even as another part warns me to run. I've imagined this moment, but it was so different. I wasn't half-naked, we weren't arguing, he hadn't just told me he'd punish me.

I want this. I want him. But I'm afraid of what will happen if he kisses me.

His lips press against mine insistently, and my warring thoughts disappear as suddenly as they came. My body heats, a fusion of light and longing and a desperate, throbbing need that builds when my lips part and his tongue meets mine. Strong fingers massage the back of my neck while his other hand strokes my thigh.

I want him. Oh, God, I want him.

A door opens. Voices coming our way.

He lets me go. I jump backward as if scorched.

What are we doing?

My cheeks burn when I hear footsteps heading this way. Thayer busies himself tidying the first aid kit when we suddenly both stare at my legs and apparently realize at the very same time that I'm not wearing any pants.

Thayer looks quickly around the room and grabs a rumpled blanket on the armchair. He throws it at me.

"Fucking cover yourself," he growls in a heated whisper.

Ugh, the *nerve* of him!

"You did it," I snap.

He gives me another look laced with the whole *if you were mine* speech.

So I do the only sensible thing. I stick my tongue out at him.

My God, what is wrong with me? If tonight has taught me anything, it's that nowhere is safe.

People are violent and untrustworthy, and Thayer has basically just said as much.

So, naturally, I kissed him.

Ugh!

Lyam enters the room with Mario Rossi as I clumsily cover my bare legs and yank my pants halfway up.

I saw both of them when I first came in but was so fraught with nerves, I barely recognized them. I remember Mario now.

Lyam doesn't even look at me. If he notices anything out of place, or if he cares, he doesn't let on.

"Get her out of here, Thayer. They haven't traced her back to us yet, so I called in some favors. They don't know where she is or who she is, but there's a posse on the prowl for the tall, pretty woman with the hot-pink hair."

Mario nods, corroborating this. "Word's already gone far and wide." He turns to me. "You were at Avelline's?"

I shrug, still blushing, but very, very thankful for that damn blanket.

"The Chaberts, Thayer," Lyam says in a low voice.

"Fuck." Thayer looks like he wants to torture, maim, and eventually kill somebody.

"You know what this means."

Lyam and Thayer stare at each other until Thayer finally nods.

"Uh, does someone want to fill me in? Because I have no idea what this means. I don't know any of these names."

I try to pretend that I'm very put together, after having fallen and scraped myself to pieces, begging hysterically for help, allowing Thayer to doctor me up, then *kissing the man*.

Very put together and grown up, indeed.

I want to sob. I want to hide.

I want him to kiss me again.

"You two tell me if anyone's in the foyer," Thayer says. When they go, he turns and hisses to me, "Get dressed."

I quickly yank my pants up over my ass and zip them just as Lyam and Mario come back.

"No one."

Mario sits beside me and gives me a look of concern. "Do you have anywhere to go?"

I swallow, my predicament suddenly seeming insurmountable. Where can I hide?

"I can't go back to America," I begin.

"Definitely not," Thayer snaps.

I frown at him and lift my chin.

If you were mine...

I draw in a deep breath and continue. "I have a flat here in Paris, which is—"

"Infinitely more dangerous than America," Thayer supplies.

I grit my teeth so I don't snap at him. Nervy bastard.

I think. I have no friends I could stay with. If I went to stay with Nicolette and Fabien, I would compromise them. I can't do that to them. It isn't fair.

"I'll... I'll have to find a place," I supply, mustering up every scrap of courage I have. I've got the money. It's just a matter of flying to somewhere far, far away, where they'll never think to find me.

"Find a place?" Lyam says with a grimace, less judgy than his brother but still obviously displeased. "Like... a hotel? Fuck that. Maman could even put you up here if necessary."

I shake my head. "I will not put anyone else in danger. And if they find out that I'm staying with your family, this will not end well."

"She's right," Mario says, nodding. "Listen, we can hide her in America. You know my family has The

Castle in New England, and multiple safe houses. No one would find her."

I blink. For how long? I can't spend the rest of my life in a safe house... apart from Nicolette again.

No.

I shake my head. "That's so generous of you," I begin, when Thayer interrupts me.

"She'll come with me."

We all stare at him.

"With you where?" Lyam asks with a wariness in his tone that makes me uneasy.

"You know where."

A slow, sly smile spreads across Mario's face.

That doesn't exactly make me feel better about things.

"Oh, yeah," Mario says. "Perfect. I mean, hardly anyone even knows it exists. You'll be near Fabien and Nicolette when they return, and a whole host of guards. You'll be damn near bulletproof, too." His eyes twinkle, and I can tell he has a few more things he isn't saying.

"Um. Hi. My name's Savannah," I say, waving my hand at them. "Not sure you remembered I was here, but I am, and my opinion matters in this."

Thayer's eyes narrow. "Of course it matters," he says. "Do you want to live or die?"

Acid burns the back of my throat.

"Why do you have to say it like that?" I ask in a little voice.

Mario sighs. "Listen, kiddo. Thayer says it like it is. Sugarcoating isn't in his vocabulary. And yeah, he can be a pain in the ass like any of us, but there's no place you'll be safer. You have to trust him."

Kiddo. Oof.

I just witnessed a murder. An unexpected, graphic, very violent murder. I don't feel like trusting anyone right now, especially not the man who said he'd punish me if I were his.

Especially not the man who has the ability to make me afraid and excited and aroused with a mere look. I could argue that's even more dangerous than the obvious situation I'm in, but I don't think they'd buy it.

"Answer the question, Savannah."

"Of course I want to live. I just… have a feeling that answering that question has strings attached."

I suddenly realize that knocking on their door—coming here for help, kissing him—has strings attached.

Thayer nods. "You're in grave danger," he says almost gently. "Tonight, you witnessed a murder, and very well might be the only witness still alive. If our suspicions are right, and I'll have you know Lyam's rarely wrong, you'll have people after you that won't just kill you. They'll kidnap you and torture you just for the hell of it before they kill you. That woman you saw? You just ruined their fun. And they won't take too kindly to that."

I stare, unblinking, trying to process the enormity of this. "So I have to hide for the rest of my life?"

"Not the rest of your life," Lyam says. "But until you're no longer in danger. We'll handle this as it plays out, but for now, your best bet is to go with Thayer. He'll take you to a place no one knows about. You'll be very well hidden. We'll make sure this blows over and that you aren't hurt."

Thayer lifts his phone and glances at the screen.

"Fabien and Nicolette have landed." He turns to me. "They've been filled in, Savannah. Do you want to talk to your sister?"

Tears spring to my eyes. I nod wordlessly and reach my hand out, swallowing hard. Thayer slides the phone into my hand. Our fingers touch for the briefest second before I pull away.

"Nicolette?" I whisper.

"Oh, thank God you're okay." My sister sounds like she's crying. "I heard what happened. Savannah, go with Thayer. Please, honey. Go with Thayer, and we'll take it from there."

I nod, even though she can't see me. All of my arguments and reasons for not going with him don't hold a candle to my sister's tearful plea. I'd do anything she asked me.

"If you want me to," I whisper.

"I do, honey. I can't talk right now," she says. "Fabien says you have to move quickly, and we can talk more when you're secure. Okay? Go, Savannah. Go *now*."

"Okay," I repeat. It's all I need to know.

Nicolette wants me to go with Thayer.

"I love you," she whispers.

"I love you, too," I whisper back.

I return the phone to Thayer, drag my shoulders back, and nod. "When do we go?"

Frowning, he looks at my hair. "Now, and the hair has to go. With hot-pink hair, you might as well have a target on your back."

I turn away from him and swallow the lump in my throat.

It isn't the hair... hair grows back. Appearances change. It's the certain knowledge that changing my hair is only the first compromise I'll have to make.

What else will he make me do?

FOUR

Thayer

I touched the Mona Lisa with my bare hands. I took my first hit like an addict and now my blood pulses with the need for more.

I shouldn't have kissed her. It was a stupid, foolish, dick move.

She tasted better than I'd imagined.

I want to kiss her again.

And again.

I want to kiss her until every nerve in her body's on fire, until she sags against me, boneless and panting and *wet*.

That first taste of forbidden fruit might be the sweetest, but that doesn't lessen the craving for more.

Fabien and Nicolette have made it clear: they don't want Savannah to know anything about Le Luxe. She's been kept in the dark up to now, and it's my job to ensure I keep her safe without revealing too much about what exactly goes on at our club.

To the outside world, Le Luxe masquerades as a luxury hotel, and that's all Savannah needs to know.

Hidden off the Ajaccio Coast, south of Paris in Corsica, the exclusive club is highly secured. Only members and curated guests are allowed through the gate, and then only after passing rigorous screening and paying a premium fee. In return, we offer luxury, state-of-the-art amenities, privacy, and top-notch security. We don't receive so much as a slip of mail without rigorous screening and documentation.

Masters and slaves, dominants and submissives, make up the bulk of our establishment. As the owner and purveyor, I have to be discriminating and selective.

But first, we have to get there, and *now*.

I keep Fabien and Nicolette abreast of every decision we make.

Me:

> Lyam and Mario are going ahead to nail down security. But I'll be the one that escorts her.

Fabien:

> Thank you.

I let Lyam and Mario go ahead of us to make sure we have an impenetrable security system in place, but *no one* will escort her but me.

I tell myself it doesn't matter, that I can do this job. I tell myself that I won't sate my craving for her.

I can be a brother to her.

Motherfucker.

Savannah watches me with wide, curious eyes, but doesn't say anything for long minutes. It's unlike her. She's usually a nonstop chatterbox. I wonder what's going on with her.

I turn to her.

"Are you afraid?"

When she flinches, I realize my tone came out harsher than I intended. Maybe that's a good thing. Maybe I need to keep her at arm's length. I fucked up kissing her, and I can't make that mistake again.

When she responds, her voice drips with sarcasm. "What gave you that idea?"

"You're not talking. That's unlike you."

I watch as she holds her head high with her chin pointed upward, as if trying to steel herself against something. Proving herself. Ready to take on the world.

Jesus, that makes me hard.

Her eyes sharpen when I look at her, as if daring anyone to take her on.

Fuck if I don't want to take that dare.

I can't.

I don't trust myself with her. I know that if I let myself loose, I'll dominate every inch of her body. I'll demand her submission. I'll make her scream with pleasure and cry in pain. I've craved the submission of a woman just like her — strong and sexy, witty and winsome.

I can't do that to her. She's too young, too innocent, and *practically family.*

I have one and only one job: to protect her no matter the cost. Even if that means denying myself everything.

I'm tormented by conflicting emotions. I clench my fists and breathe in through my nostrils.

She doesn't deserve my anger. *She* isn't the one I'm angry with.

I tell myself I need to push her away. Savannah is too trusting.

Too innocent.

"Maybe I have nothing to say."

"Unlikely."

I snap my mouth shut in an effort to keep myself from snapping at her again.

"Okay, then, maybe I do have something to say but I don't want to say it to *you*."

I turn to face her this time. Her eyes meet mine—so gorgeous, my heart turns in my chest. She's curious, and if I'm not mistaken, a little aroused.

I tamp down the urge to set things straight. To tell her my expectations. To discuss hard limits.

I'll never be one to go for a modern relationship. It's not who I am.

The first time I discovered I'm a dominant, I felt as if a whole world opened up to me. Fabien was the one who took me to a club in Paris. The first night there I knew. This was where I belonged.

I need to be the one in charge. I'm the one who needs to protect. To command.

Call it old-fashioned, but I know who I am. I know what I like. I know what I need.

My job is to protect her, no matter the cost.

Even if she hates me.

I open my mouth to respond, to tell her off. I snap it shut again.

She isn't mine.

If Savannah was mine...

My phone rings. I glance down. Lyam.

"Yeah?"

"Coast clear. Let's go."

I jerk my chin at her. "Come here."

I take a quick minute to send Lyam a text. I'll need a few things for this trip.

"I really wish you'd learn to treat me half decently," she snaps.

I turn to her and imagine what it would be like to hold her down, strip her, and fuck her until she doesn't have a single thread of resistance left in her.

I swallow the urge and reach for her.

"My job is to keep you alive," I tell her honestly. "I don't care what the fuck I have to do to make that happen. You're not mine, Savannah, and we've covered what that would look like if you were." I close the mental door on that fantasy so quickly it splinters. "But your sister and brother-in-law have asked me to take care of you. That's exactly what I'm going to do."

"Maybe," she seethes through gritted teeth, "I don't want your protection."

Without thinking, I take hold of her wrists and pin them to her sides.

Upstairs, a door opens. I hear the gentle padding of light footsteps.

"Lyam? Thayer?"

Maman.

She can't see us from here, but she likely can't sleep, either, knowing that Savannah's in danger.

I yell over my shoulder, holding Savannah's gaze. "We're leaving now, Maman. I'll fill you in later."

Savannah's eyes spark fire. "Tell him to be nice to me, Mrs. Gerard!" she yells. Of all the—

"Thayer doesn't listen to me, darling!" Maman yells. "But you'll be safe with him, I promise! Just do what he tells you, he'll do anything to keep you safe."

I give her a triumphant look.

"Her, too?" she says in a heated whisper.

I give her a look that says *I told you so*.

"You don't have to be so rough," she protests.

"Savannah," I whisper in her ear. "If you think this is rough, lovely, you have no idea what I'm capable of."

"Oh, bragging now, are we?" But the pink blush on her cheeks gives her away. She looks at me as if she's too proud to admit she wants to know just exactly what *rough* can be.

Her torn clothing's so thin and flimsy, I can see the outline of her breasts. When I touch her skin, goosebumps erupt, as if I'm drawing an uncontrollable reaction from her. I can feel her pulse pounding against my fingers.

She smells of roses.

The car's waiting. Her pursuers may have discovered her identity, if not her whereabouts. We need to go.

"From now on," I say in a slow, measured tone, "you're under my protection. You gave up any control when you walked through that door."

"What exactly is that supposed to mean?" I wonder if I imagine the curiosity that sparks in her eyes.

I pull her closer to me. "It means I expect you to obey me. Even though I don't own you, your choice to seek my protection means there are consequences for disobedience." Heat flares between us, a fusion of anger and arousal, fury and need. The reality of her situation seems to strike her all at once, as her mouth parts. I stare at her lips. I want to lick them, bite them, stroke my tongue against hers until she moans. "I want to make this very clear, Savannah. I'll do whatever it takes to keep you safe. Do you understand me?"

Her jaw opens in protest. Closes and swallows. Finally she shakes her head and snaps, "You are so full of yourself." She presses her lips together as she glares at me and likely weighs her options.

I have no more patience.

"I didn't ask you your opinion of me. I asked if you understood. Now, either tell me you do, or we start over, and this time, we'll have this discussion with you over my knee."

This time, her outrage is unmistakable. Her breathing quickens as she apparently plays this all out in her mind.

She might hate me, but maybe she likes the idea of being over my knee.

When she speaks, her voice is low and throaty.

Angry, or... aroused?

"I'm not stupid," she protests.

"I never said you were."

"And yet you insist on treating me as if I am."

I shake my head. "Not true. I never said you were stupid, and I wouldn't think that."

Jesus, I think she's brilliant.

"Then why would you think I'd do something that put me in danger? You're talking as if I have no concept of self-preservation. It's why I came here."

I draw in a breath and let it out slowly. Patience isn't really my thing.

"Because you've never been where we're going. You don't know the people we're dealing with."

I can feel her breath on my skin. We're too close. *Too close.*

"And you do?" she snaps.

"Yes. And there are a few things I know. First, the people who committed this murder aren't the type to let this go. They will follow you. They already have a search party out, and they won't let this go until they find you."

She licks her lips and nods. I stifle a groan.

Why does she lick her lips? God!

"Second. If you report them, their leader goes to jail. There will be trials and interviews and you'll be in a spotlight. It's very much in their interest to make sure you don't repeat what you saw, and they'll find the most expedient way possible to make sure that doesn't happen."

"Alright." Her voice trembles.

"We're going to a place that's not found on any map. You'll be safe there."

She eyes me warily. "Does your mother know about this?"

Why does she insist on bringing my mother into the situation?

"No."

She gives me a look of disapproval I ignore.

"We're driving to the airport. We're flying to an undisclosed location. For parts of this, you'll be blindfolded." She slow-blinks. "We'll discuss more on our flight, but we leave *now*. We're walking out that door to a ride that's waiting for us. And if you do anything other than walk out that door with me, I will pick you up and carry you out bodily." I let out a breath. "Don't make me do that, Savannah."

I don't give her time to protest, talk, or ask questions. I walk briskly to the door, taking her along with me. "I'm only going because your mother told me you'd keep me safe," she says, as if to make it very clear that there's no way in hell she'd do this of her own accord.

"Then why didn't you go to the police? Why did you come here?"

She has no answer for that.

I know exactly why she came here. The police can't offer the type of protection I can.

The police are bound by laws.

Lyam hands me a bag with a wig he probably got from Fabien's expansive collection. We'll have to cut and dye her hair—the most distinguishing characteristic she has—but for now, the wig will do.

"You ever worn a wig before?"

She makes a sound of disgust. "No."

"Stand still, then. It might get itchy, but you'll only wear this until we can change your hair color more effectively."

I pull her against my chest and make short work of tucking the silky strands of pink under the wig. That quickly, Savannah becomes a brunette with full, straight brown hair that graces her shoulders.

It looks amazing on her. *Jesus*. Everything does. I could make her bald, and she'd still make me ache for her.

When we exit the house, Mario and Lyam flank our sides, weapons drawn. She takes in an audible breath at the flash of gunmetal gray on either side.

I draw my own weapon as well.

As one unit, we walk to the car, our steps in sync. In silence.

Even Savannah stays quiet and walks quickly to the armored car idling by the curb.

I open the door and gesture for her to go in first, then slide in beside her. Lyam takes the driver's seat and Mario goes to sit in the passenger seat.

"Maman's secure," Lyam says as he puts the car in drive and begins to head toward the airport. "We've called for heightened security measures."

I nod.

"Lyam, did you alert her team?"

"I did."

It's a somber ride, but a fast one. We're close enough we could walk but it's safer to drive.

"I didn't pack anything," Savannah says. She turns away from me, and I wonder why. Even from here I can see a lone tear roll down her cheek.

It's been a long night for her.

"We'll get what you need."

She nods.

"What about my apartment?" She turns to me, not bothering to hide the tears on her cheeks. "I have a fish, Thayer."

Fish. Her life is in danger, and she's worried about her fish.

"I'll make sure it's fed," I say with practiced patience.

She looks back out the window. "Alright."

We make it to the airport, surrounded by security. Armored cars follow behind, flank each side, and ride ahead of us as well.

"Where are we going?"

"I can't tell you that."

She rolls her eyes. "Is this one of those 'If I tell you I'd have to kill you' speeches?"

Of all the disrespectful things—

I silence her with a look. She gives me the middle finger. Mario actually gasps. Lyam chuckles and reaches into his pocket before he casually slides me what I asked him for. I put the sleek package in my pocket.

I narrow my eyes at her. Oh, I'll remember that.

I'm not sure why she's so angry with me. I'm not the one that put her in this predicament.

Finally, I break the silence with a question that's been plaguing me for a little while. "Why didn't you have your guard with you?"

"Oh, God, you too?"

"Me, too, what?"

"Fabien and Nicolette have been on my ass about getting guards."

I close my eyes briefly, willing myself not to snap again. "Do you mean to tell me," I say slowly, "that you don't have any guards?"

Her sheepish grimace is all the answer I need.

"Savannah!"

"Seriously, that's exactly what Fabien and Nicolette were saying, and I don't need to hear it all over again."

"Are you serious right now?"

"Fucking hell," Mario says, his eyes wide. "Savannah, there isn't a woman in my family who's allowed to brush her teeth without a damn guard."

Lyam nods. "I'm shocked Fabien allowed this."

"Guards are for special people. Celebrities?" she says, as if that explains anything. "Rich people. Not people like *me*. And I'm not actually Fabien's sister, so he has no say. And this is ridiculous because I'm not someone anyone would even target."

"Wrong. Your sister married into the Gerard family. That alone puts you at risk."

She lets out a sigh worthy of an award. "Fine. Alright. After this I have to admit I do need a guard, so I guess you all will have your way."

The rest of the trip goes off without a hitch. We land, and she scans the horizon for any sign of where we are. Though she's familiar with Corsica, she won't know our exact destination.

I wait until we're safely seated in our escort car, Mario and Lyam in a separate car to follow us, before I lay down the laws she won't like.

"Now, we talk."

Savannah eyes me warily. She's as squashed in the corner of the car as possible, her arms crossed over her chest like a child.

She needs someone to break through that exterior. Break down her defenses. Break through that resistance.

I wonder how she'd react to a spanking.

I don't know how long I'll have her, but we will find out.

"I'm going to blindfold you before we go in."

"Oooh, kinky, are we?" She's trying to be witty or funny, but I can only shake my head.

"Oh, Savannah. Love. You have no idea."

"You can't—do you—I mean, if you—" She pauses. *"Thayer."*

"Savannah."

"Don't say my name like that," she whispers, then looks away quickly, as if regretting what she just said. Shaking her head, she grimaces. "Forget I said that."

Why does she ask me that? Why doesn't she want me to say her name? It's a strange request.

I love her name. It's old-fashioned, feminine, and beautiful... all the things I like best about her.

"Like I said, it's time to talk," I begin. "I'm taking you to an exclusive club. At this club, clients pay very high-end prices for anonymity and privacy. Only certain members are allowed entry. You'll likely... see things that might be a little... foreign to you."

She eyes me with suspicion. "What do you mean? And how do you know what I have and have not seen? Is this like some kind of kinky sex club?"

There's no hiding the truth, so I nod. "Something like that."

"Ahhh," she says, nodding with a little grin. "Really?" she drawls in a classic Southern Belle imitation. "Why, Thayer. I had no idea."

I blow out a stream of breath and turn away. "I know."

I need this woman alone, in private, and *now*.

"My, my," she says with a teasing glint in her eyes. "What else do you hide behind that tough exterior?" She reaches for my hand and strokes her thumb along the top of it. My dick twitches and my pulse spikes. *Fucking hell.*

Tough exterior, eh? I'll show her tough exterior—

"Savannah." I lace my voice with warning, but she doesn't seem to care. She turns fully to face me, as if she's completely oblivious to the fact that she's in danger and this is no joking matter.

"All this time," she says in a low voice. "All this time, you've been hiding these secrets..."

That does it.

In one swift move, I grab her by the waist and pin her against me, so her back is to my chest and my left arm's solidly in place around her. I reach in my pocket for the package from Lyam—a slim blindfold and supple restraints. With a firm grip, I loop the satiny restraint around her wrists and pull tight.

"Oh, we're kinky alright," she says, though her lilting voice doesn't hide the flash of alarm in her eyes.

I ignore her while I slide the blindfold over her eyes.

"This is for your own good," I whisper, as I tie it at the back of her head.

"Ah. That's what they all say."

I grit my teeth. "Should've brought a gag."

FIVE

Savannah

Oh, I talk a good talk alright. It's the only way I can gain any control over a situation which threatens to unravel at any moment.

But it doesn't mean my heart isn't threatening to leap out of my chest. It doesn't mean I'm not wildly curious about where he's taking me or how exactly he just happens to have a blindfold and some kind of rope in his pocket.

He planned this.

Yeah, he mentioned something about me being blindfolded so I wouldn't see where I was going, but I suspect he has a dual purpose. I mean, he's basically said as much. Is he *really* just trying to make sure I don't know my whereabouts?

I really don't have the first clue about where we're going.

My older sister and I need to have a nice long talk.

As soon as the silky blindfold darkens my vision, my other senses come alive.

I can feel the warm, hard wall of his chest against my back. I'm enveloped in the utterly masculine scent of whatever the hell he's wearing that says *Male. Sex. Power.*

Gah! I try to speak but find my mouth's too dry. When I lick my lips, I hear him stifle a groan.

I wonder why.

I can hear the low hum of the engine. I imagine I hear the drumming beat of my heart. A whisper of a shiver runs between my shoulder blades when his mouth brushes my ear.

"We're almost there. Listen, and do not speak. Nod if you understand."

God, the arrogance of this son of a bitch. "What's there not to understand?" I snap.

Strong fingers at my neck flex. I gasp. He wouldn't —choke me—would he?

He bites my ear. I gasp and writhe, but he holds me fast.

"No more attitude. No more talking back. I don't know what you think's so funny about this, but you are two breaths away from having your ass whipped over my knee, no matter *where* we are, no matter *who* sees. Do you understand *that*?"

I nod and open my mouth to speak again, when he continues.

"This is not a joke. You're in serious danger. I'm bringing you into an exclusive club where people go who will not think twice about me dragging you in there cuffed, blindfolded, gagged, and trussed up for my use. Where not a single soul will even blink if I take my belt to your ass and punish you for disobedience. Where everyone, and I mean literally everyone, will step aside to give me a wide berth the second they see who I am. Where my word is law and my command absolute. Is *that* clear, Savannah?"

Ho-ly. *Shit!*

I nod.

Where the hell is he taking me?

And more importantly... who the hell *is* he?

"You'll walk beside me. You'll stay silent except to answer my questions if I speak to you. I'll bring you to my private suite and then you can have more freedom, but until then, you are nothing more than my property."

His. Property.

I should be appalled.

I'm actually a little appalled that I'm *not* appalled.

I'm more curious than anything.

I'd like to see him keep his hands off me under *these* circumstances. Ha!

Nicolette would only shake her head.

Nicolette.

Surely Fabien and Nicolette know where we're going. Why have they never mentioned anything to me before? Do they all think I'm a child or something? I'm in grad school, for crying out loud. I've moved to another continent and learned the language, earned a massive scholarship for grad school, and have even, though Nicolette doesn't know this yet, written three mystery thrillers. Okay, so they're not published yet, but I'm getting there. I want to know I'm able to do it on my own, without the help of Fabien and Nicolette.

It sounds like Thayer's either talking on the phone or giving instructions to someone, I can't quite tell which. But I tell my overactive imagination to take a breather and start paying attention either way.

We've stopped moving, that much I can tell. Voices, speaking in rapid French at a bit of a distance, move past us and come back. God, I wish I could *see*. What do they look like when they see Thayer?

My word is law and my command absolute.

What does that mean? And why does it make my body come *alive*?

"Savannah." Again, he says my name. Again, when he does, I wish he'd say it again.

I shouldn't care about him any more now that I know what an asshole he can be. It was a lot easier to be hot for him and fuel my schoolgirl fantasies when I didn't know that he was sarcastic and rude and bossy.

I also didn't know how well he kissed, either.

Or how hard his body was.

Or how good he smelled.

Gah!

I try to will myself to remember he can be callous and impolite. But a part of me wonders if it isn't just an act. Why would he kiss me if he isn't attracted to me? Would a guy like him go out of his way to protect me on mere principle?

The more I try to resist him, the more I find myself longing for more.

I want to see what it's like to be with a man whose "word is law and command absolute."

He's already blindfolded and tied me up and threatened to spank me. He laughed at my reference to kink. And what the hell kind of a place is frequented by people who don't care about things like... potential servitude?

"We're here. From now on, you'll pretend that you're mine, Savannah."

Why does my throat ache at that?

I'm afraid to ask the question but can't help it.

"Your... what?"

He releases a harsh breath. "My slave."

What?

The flare of alarm quickly fades when he brushes his lips across the naked skin at my collarbone.

I close my eyes behind the blindfold and brace against the sudden rush of heat and warmth and need. *I want to be beneath him. I want to feel him slide into me. I want to feel his naked skin against mine. I want him to break me, then put me back together again, bit by bit.*

Wait. Maybe sometimes I let my writer's imagination get the best of me.

Surely, he didn't say *slave*.

As in... like, captive. Bond servant. Serf. Servant?

Property?

I must have misheard him.

"Ha! So I thought you said *slave*," I snort.

"I did."

I open my mouth to say something else, when I hear him mutter, "Goddamn, I can't believe I didn't bring a gag."

Holy hell, this guy has cast-iron rocks.

"I'm going to open that door. The second I do, you're my slave. We'll talk about what that means later, but for now it means you're in complete and utter submission to me. Your one and only job is to listen and obey. Yeah, you can give me that mouthy master bullshit speech later, which I'm sure you're just dying to do. For now, you do what I tell you without question, and you'll make it to my bedroom without earning yourself a punishment session."

My cheeks heat, but I have no time to process this when I hear the unmistakable sound of a door opening. I swallow hard when hushed voices welcome him in French.

Who knew the beautiful language could make even slavery sound classy?

Thayer doesn't bother with formalities or politeness, but issues commands in a harsh, authoritative voice. Though they speak in French, I understand them easily.

"Is my room ready?"

"Yes, sir, of course, sir."

"Thank you. Do we have any new arrivals?"

"No, sir. We have closed our doors to new visitors since we received your call and sent notifications that we will not be receiving new guests until further notice."

He's practically holding me beside him as we walk at a brisk pace. I shiver when a cold gust of wind tickles my neck. Without a word, he tucks me closer to him, so I'm pressed against the warmth of his body while he continues the interrogation and quick pace.

"Very good. Have all security staff been called?"

"Yes, sir."

It's late at night, the wee hours of the morning, I'm guessing, yet his staff members are ready to listen and obey.

Interesting.

I hear the unmistakable sound of a door opening and closing. Hushed voices. The rush of falling water. My heels click on the smooth, slippery floor —marble?—before quickly muting when my feet sink into plush carpet. Classical music plays on speakers seemingly all around us, beautiful but achingly sad. The scent of mint and lavender permeates the air around us, as if we're in a luxury spa.

"Ah, Thayer. Didn't expect you back so soon."

"Didn't know I'd be back." The tone of his voice gives me the impression he isn't super cool about talking to this person.

"And who might your guest be? Did you bring a toy to share for once?"

"Touch her," Thayer says in a pleasant voice laced with ice, "and I'll break your hand."

My pulse spikes.

"Ooh, violence," the nameless voice responds. "Rumor has it you can be violent when the situation warrants it, but I didn't know you'd be so easily provoked." The dark chuckle sends an unpleasant shiver down my spine. I imagine the person he's talking to dressed in a snake's skin.

"I will not be sharing," Thayer snaps, implying the utter and instant death of whoever might question him otherwise.

"Understood. But if you change your mind, you know where to find me."

"I'm not changing my mind."

The chuckle continues.

The retreating footsteps assure me whoever's expressed an interest in me has gone.

Thayer curses and walks us a few more paces forward.

"And this is why," Thayer says in a low voice to me, "we should've hired another manager."

"What do you mean?"

"You've received my messages?" Thayer asks someone. No answer to my question, then.

"Yes, sir. Of course, sir."

"Perfect."

We turn to leave and begin walking at a rapid pace, and I get the distinct impression he wants to get me out of here as fast as he can, but he still has business to tend to.

"And sir?"

Thayer doesn't slow his pace at all. "Yes?"

"We've prepared everything you asked us to for your ten o'clock meeting tomorrow."

We come to such a sudden, screeching halt, I would have stumbled if he didn't brace me against him with an arm around my waist.

"Excuse me?"

That tone of his voice sends another shiver down my spine. I imagine whoever he's talking to has backed up against a wall.

"Your guests, sir?"

Thayer's still beside me. "I didn't invite any guests. I have no idea what you're talking about." He curses under his breath.

"We received a message this morning, requesting the security and privacy of room two. We've temporarily asked all willing servants to relocate to the playroom."

My. Head. Is. Spinning.

Willing servants?

The playroom?

"Is that right?" Thayer asks in a low voice. "One minute, please."

He shifts, and I hear the gentle rustle of clothes. I imagine he's looking for his phone. It's strange standing here in the dark like this.

"Let me look into this," he finally says. "Thank you for updating me. I'm sorry there's been a change of plans, but I appreciate your attention to this matter. It must've slipped my mind."

I don't believe him. He's lying. Thayer is too much of a perfectionist to forget something like this.

They continue their conversation and finally, he says goodbye.

We walk past a room with muffled voices. Another where a warm rush of air, scented like warmed vanilla, kisses my skin before we move past. It seems we're walking down a hall of sorts.

We come to a stop. I hear a beep as he pushes what must be an elevator button, and seconds later, the rush of opening doors.

"Thayer!"

A woman's voice makes him stop. I feel him turning around. His grip on me slackens.

"Camille." I wish I could see his face. His tone is hard to read.

"How *are* you?" she asks.

Camille... oh my God, if that's the *model* Camille...

I can't be jealous. I shouldn't be jealous. I need to shut off the part of my brain that's justifying my jealousy.

Instead of answering, he asks her an odd question. "Why are you out here unescorted? Didn't they read you the rules?"

"I'm alone," she says in a breathy whisper.

Oh, ew. Are we playing that game?

"Unescorted."

"Really."

"I know," she says, in a tone that would melt butter, "it's hard for you to believe that I don't have an escort, isn't it? But some of us like being free," she continues. "And who's your blindfolded guest? She looks... lovely."

The tone of her voice says she does not think I look lovely at all. I suddenly remember my tousled hair, the torn and rumpled clothing that's been through hell and back.

"She's exactly what you said. My guest."

"Ah, no name?"

I half expect him to say my name is *Slave X* or something.

"If you'll excuse us, we've had a long day and are looking forward to a good night's sleep."

"Oh, of course. Don't let me be rude and hold you up." Even blindfolded—maybe especially blindfolded—I note the biting edge to her tone. "Enjoy your evening, both of you. *Au revoir!*"

Her heels click on the floor as she leaves.

"Motherfucker," he mutters under his breath. "I am going to kill him. Seriously, kill him."

Who? What?

I could write a book with the number of questions I have right about now.

I press my lips together and gesture to my lips.

The air's heavy with foreboding as he draws closer to me.

"Yes," he snaps. "Still not talking. Go ahead, love. Try me." My insides clench even as my heart thunders. Dread washes through me when I realize he's looking for a reason to punish me.

Oh, well then. Apparently, he's looking for a reason to punish me.

Why do I like it when he calls me *love*? He doesn't mean it. I'm confident he's only being sarcastic.

Not sure how I feel about the threat. To say I have mixed feelings would be an understatement.

He leads me forward, and when I hear the sliding doors of an elevator again, I imagine we've made it inside. We begin going upward.

I have so many questions, and I'm not quite sure it's *right* that he thinks he can punish me… but he's also the one with the major advantage here.

In other words, I'm not gonna rock this boat.

Yet, anyway.

If Thayer Gerard thinks he can boss me around without consequence, then do I ever have a surprise for him. *This* girl is no pushover. And while being overpowered and dominated by him—and yes, maybe even punished—might appeal to me on some base, primal level, I won't forget who I am. What I've been through.

What I want.

And I will not just roll over and beg like a well-trained dog.

I don't care how hot he is. I don't care that he's rich, and that deep down inside, a part of me craves his protection. I've been alone for a very long time, and even though I like having control over my own life... it gets lonely.

So I don't care who he is or what he does. This whole slave thing might be a part of the disguise I'll use to save my life... but that's all this is. A cloak to hide me. Trickery. Playacting.

No one is safe from a man like Thayer. Especially me.

"I'm putting you in a suite," he says.

That sounds promising.

I want to ask if I'll be alone or if he'll join me, but I don't want to sound too eager. And honestly, I'm not even sure I *want* him to be with me.

I might want him in the moment—just like I might stress-eat a box of chocolates all by myself—but will it be worth it in the morning?

Will I have to lose too much of myself to really stay safe?

Is safety only an illusion?

SIX

Thayer

I don't trust that things are going as planned.

Someone fucked up. Maybe even played me.

I didn't call for a meeting. I have no guests arriving. I don't forget things like that.

So I'm distracted when I lead Savannah to the private suite I've planned to take her to.

"Hey," Savannah whispers.

I sigh. I will never bring this girl out in public again without a gag. She's going to end up over my knee before she goes to bed tonight.

"What did I tell you about talking?" I say in a low voice. "Is this an emergency?"

"Does having to pee qualify as an emergency?" she asks, tipping her head adorably even while blindfolded.

I grit my teeth. "Do you have to use the bathroom?"

"Well, no, but I wondered."

"Savannah." She flinches as if I struck her.

"Why do you talk to me like that?" she hisses.

"Like what?"

"Like you're scolding me as if I'm a child."

"Because you're acting like a child," I hiss back.

Her jaw drops as if she's shocked. "I am not! That isn't true."

I'm in a club that I own and manage. I'm a well-respected dominant and master, who's just brought in a woman masquerading as my slave. If she makes anyone suspect that she isn't truly my slave, she'll put herself in danger. It's a red flag.

I could punish her right here. I could take my belt to her ass and make her obey. I will, but now isn't the time. Right now, I need her to stop talking. And if she won't obey me on her own, I'll have to make her.

I pause long enough to untie her hands, but only so I can remove her top.

"Hey!"

I flick it over her head, twist it into a rope, then loop it around her mouth. With her hands free, she slaps at my arms to stop me. I restrain her wrists and pull them behind her back. When they're secured, I bend her over my knee and give her a handful of good, hard spanks.

"The next time you raise your hand to me, I'll bare your ass before I punish you," I say, nice and loud for anyone nearby to hear.

I stand her upright, fully aware of her protests mumbled under the gag as I drag her along.

We need privacy, and now. It's been a long, long night and neither of us is in the mood to drag this out any longer than it needs to be.

The right thing to do would be to put her in a suite under high security, with monitors and a team of guards.

I don't always do the right thing. Hell, I rarely do the right thing.

I open the door while she chatters on and on behind the gag. I shut and lock it. With decades of experience under my belt, I would've thought I could handle her protests better than I have.

I let her get under my skin.

I scan the room and make a call.

"I want six guards stationed outside my suite."

"Yes, sir. Of course, sir."

I hang up the phone. It's not out of the ordinary that we have a high-profile guest. It's one of the reasons why Le Luxe is so exclusive and profitable. We charge a premium for security and anonymity, including having well-equipped guards available at a moment's notice. The public playrooms have guards in every corner, and we screen our clients so carefully, we've never had so much as a single incident of misconduct.

I let out a breath. Finally.

We're alone.

I imagined this.

Savannah tied up and ready for my use. At my command. Ready to be mastered.

Only in my fantasy, she was here because she wanted to be, not spitting mad like a feral cat.

"We're alone now. This room is soundproof and remote. We have guards stationed outside. You're safe."

Her shoulders relax a tiny bit.

"Now that we're alone, we have to set a few things straight. I'm going to take off your blindfold, restraints, and gag."

I don't give her an ultimatum.

Yet.

First, the blindfold.

Light smolders in her beautiful eyes, even as they snap at me. Unfathomable beauty, intelligence, and brilliance all spark in her eyes. I long to soften her gaze. To soothe her anger. To bring out the submissive I know lurks inside her.

She's still gagged and bound, so I take a minute to admire her.

"You look lovely as a brunette," I murmur.

"Mmpph."

I pretend I know exactly what she says. "Very clever. And you're welcome."

"*Mmmph!*"

I won't waste any more of my time or hers. It's time to make this woman obey me. She needs to learn her place, for her own damn good.

I grab the knot at the back of her head so I can unfasten the gag. "Now listen, Savannah," I whisper in her ear, "I'm talking this gag off. There will be plenty of time for you to ask me questions and for us to talk. But it's late, and we need to get to bed. It's best if we get some sleep and discuss this in the morning. You need to understand, though. We're here for your safety. And to make this work, you need to be sure that you're in your role. Your role here is my slave. You'll obey me. If you don't, I'll punish you."

I whip off the gag.

"How many times are you going to say that?" she seethes.

I grab her chin in my hand and squeeze. Her eyes widen. "As many times as it fucking takes."

"You are so full of yourself," she says through clenched teeth.

"Your point?"

"Argh!"

"Now whether or not you go to bed with a sore ass is up to you. You're not mine. We've covered what that means. But since you're under my protection and in my care, I'll hold you to certain standards."

She nods with narrowed eyes.

"I'll expect you to show respect to me. I'll expect you to defer to my authority and do what I say. I'll expect you to submit yourself to discipline, and for all intents and purposes, behave like my slave when we're out in public."

"And in private?"

"In private, you'll treat me like the fucking man who's going to save your life. Got it?"

Though she still fumes, she knows there's no way she can get away with anything now. We're in my home. We're on my terms. She's under my protection. And Savannah's a smart girl.

She heaves out a sigh. "Got it."

I wonder if she's as innocent and pure as I suspect.

Is she a virgin?

I can't help but wonder if a part of her, deep down, wants this. Does she know how intensely erotic it can be?

I wonder if she can feel the way I'm mentally undressing her. Dominating her. Envisioning her parted lips and tortured plea, begging for me to allow her to come as lust trumps her protests and she grows desperate—

I can't do this.

Fuck all.

She's Nicolette's sister.

My own angry gaze meets hers as I reach for the restraints at her wrists.

"Behave yourself when I unfasten these. They were for show at first, but now I want to be completely sure you don't do anything that will jeopardize us."

"Fine," she grates out. "I won't."

I want to tease her a little more while she's still under my control.

"Ask me nicely."

"You son of a bitch—"

"Savannah." She clamps her lips shut at the warning in my tone.

I hold her hands in mine. "I said," I repeat, holding her gaze. "Ask me nicely."

"Or you'll just leave me bound like this?"

"Yes."

"Ha!" she says humorlessly, despite the look of triumph in her eyes. "You know you can't." She thrusts her chin in the air, as if to defy me. "How will I *wipe my ass?*"

I thread my fingers through her hair and cup the back of her head in my palm. "I've had slaves cuffed and bound for days," I say in a low voice. "Trust me. You find a way to do what you have to. It's nowhere near out of the question."

I watch as the glint of victory in her eyes fades. When she licks her lips, I find myself staring, enraptured. Her mouth is perfect, so fucking perfect.

Begging to be defiled.

I tighten my grip on her hair until she hisses in a breath and tips her head back. She stifles a little cry.

"You don't know what you're playing with, Savannah," I whisper. I kiss her cheek, her nose, her temple. When her eyes flutter closed, I kiss her lids, then tip her head down so I can kiss her forehead. With a finger under her chin, I lift her face to meet mine and brush my lips across each cheek before I move my mouth to the side of her jaw. I kiss my way down her neck to where her pulse quickens, then lick my way from her neck to her collarbone, to the valley between her breasts.

I reach for her wrists and tug them backward. Her perfect, round breasts heave when she tightens her shoulder blades. I bend down and kiss the hardened buds of her nipples through her top.

With every taste of her, the part of my conscience that tells me to stop grows harder and harder to hear.

Fabien will kill me.

I push the thought away as quickly as it comes.

Fabien who?

I tug the restraints at her wrists and pull them off in one firm motion.

I expect her to shove me away, but she doesn't. Hesitating at first, she finally wraps her arms around my neck. I groan in her ear before I can stop myself. The way she feels is perfection, like she was meant to be here.

"How much of this do you want to try, Thayer?" she whispers in my ear.

She doesn't want this. She doesn't even know what it *means* to submit to me. Savannah's innocent and naïve, and only a bastard would take advantage of her.

I never said I was a good man.

I suspect that her curiosity is what makes her say this, and that if she really knew what she was asking she would run.

Savannah's under my protection.

She's in my club.

"Try?" I reply, my voice thick with lust. My need for her overrides everything. "This isn't a game. We're not playing, Savannah." I spread my hands across her thighs, pulling her to me. She makes a low sound of approval that only spurs me on. "While you're here, you're mine. I won't risk anyone finding out who you are or putting you in danger because they suspect who you really are." I pull back just enough that I can look in her eyes.

"What does it mean to be a slave?" she whispers.

"It depends on who's the master."

Her beautiful eyes stare at me. She licks her lips.

"What does it mean to be *your* slave?" she amends.

I cup the back of her head and hold her gaze. I want her to know this. To *feel* this. "It means that I take care of you. It means that you do everything I say, not just because I like control but because I take care of your every need. It means you embrace serving me, and I serve you by taking control." I run my thumb along her lower lip, memorizing the soft, warm feel of her skin. I want to taste her so badly my mouth waters. "It means that I expect complete obedience. That you are subject to my discipline if you disobey."

She doesn't speak. I take her wrists in my hands to massage where the restraints bit into her until her flesh is warm to the touch.

She licks her lips and swallows. Fear? Apprehension?

Desire?

"If I don't pretend to be your slave, people will know I don't belong here."

I nod. "Yes." Even though I want her, even though I *crave* her, this much is true.

"They know what you do in private?"

I pause so I think before I give her my honest answer. I won't lie to her. "They don't. But submission isn't something you can just put on and take off, Savannah. The more you practice, the better you'll get. If you're only obedient to me in public, the ruse will be up."

One of us will slip.

She quirks an eyebrow up at me. "Are you sure you're not just saying that so you can do whatever the fuck you want with me?"

I feel a slow smile spread across my face. "Not at all."

SEVEN

SAVANNAH

This is maybe getting out of hand, and fast. I'm trying to think of how to respond, but I'm having a hard time keeping my thoughts logical.

When he first took my blindfold off, the first thing I did was glare at him, like I've wanted to do since he started getting all domineering with me, which was pretty much the first second I was in his presence.

Now, however, I really want to observe this place.

It's hard to keep my head on straight, though, because how am I supposed to think rationally when my body's on *fire*?

I want this, and I don't even know what "this" is. I can see the way he restrains himself, as if he's holding himself back from everything he wants to do to me.

I don't want him to hold back. I want to see what he can do, even if that means he'll destroy me.

But God, even sex-craving doesn't give me the energy I need. Right now, half the reason I'm leaning against him is because I'm so damn exhausted my eyes hurt when I blink. I lean my body against him because it's getting harder to stand.

I stifle a yawn, and he shakes his head.

"Jesus," he curses under his breath. "You must be completely exhausted. I'm an asshole."

I raise my eyebrows and don't respond, because... he isn't wrong. He *is* an asshole, but not because he's forgotten it's nearly daylight out and we've almost pulled an all-nighter.

"Come here," he says roughly. Taking me by the hand, he pulls me into the center of the room. I want to take in every detail, from the luxurious strands of lights that form a sort of chandelier over the bed, to the velvety curtains that give us privacy, the enormous bed that sits dead center in the room, elegantly draped in fine fabrics and piles of pillows.

The little hooks mysteriously screwed into the bedposts that make my heart beat a little faster.

It's like some sordid, luxurious, opulent hotel, and I want to see *everything*.

This really can't be called a room. It's closer to a flat one might find in Paris, or at the very least, a luxury suite, given its huge, walk-in closet, enormous bathroom with a tub the size of a small swimming pool, and an office that juts out on an elevated platform behind the bed. The kitchen area's also large and spacious, equipped for entertaining guests and for businesspeople to conduct business

A few days ago, I would've lost my shit if you'd told me I'd be alone in a swanky room with threats of a spanking from the likes of Thayer Gerard.

But my eyes are becoming too heavy to keep open. My body begs me to rest, and that bed looks so inviting.

"I considered giving you your own private suite, but I think that's a bullshit idea. I need to be nearby in case anything happens."

"What will Fabien say?" I ask on a yawn.

"He'd kill me if he knew I left you unattended."

"He'd kill you if he knew you tried to seduce me."

"That, too."

"A bit of a conundrum," I say on yet another yawn.

Now, though... here I am.

I walk into the bathroom and quickly scan it, looking for something to wash up with. I find the room well-appointed and comfortable, also as luxurious as before, but I'm so tired I don't even bother to take in the details.

In a sort of exhausted stupor, I sleep-wash my face and sleep-brush my teeth, then sleep-brush my hair. When I come back into the room, I find a pair of delicate, satin ivory shorts and a tank lying on the bed.

Thayer's on the phone in the office. He jerks his chin at the clothes.

He's commanded so much, I figure it can't hurt to take back a little of the control.

"*Mine?*" I whisper, gesturing at the clothes. I'm so tired, do I have to change?

He nods. "Yes," he mouths.

I could get dressed in the bathroom. Or... I could give him a little bit of a strip show.

That thought wakes me up a little.

He's had a lot of fun bossing me around, or so it seems.

Let's show him what he's missed out on.

I paste an innocent expression on my face, as if I'm not fully aware that he's about ten feet away from me, completely dressed and on the phone.

I yawn and stretch, pushing my breasts out, my eyes closed. Pretending he isn't here. That he isn't running his eyes up and down the length of my body.

I run my fingers through my hair and arch my shoulders, then stretch my neck from side to side.

I run my finger along the hem of my bra and yawn again.

I can feel him still.

Next, I unzip my pants and shove them down my legs. I ignore the wince of pain when the fabric rubs against my scratches. Step out of the jeans. Toss those, too, to the basket. Just in case he hasn't seen it yet, I pretend like I need to turn around so he can get a better view of my ass.

I stretch so he can see me fully.

Oh, what is that on the floor? An invisible speck of fluff. I bend over and pick it up so he gets nothing but the perfect view of my ass.

Smack!

I didn't see it coming. I quickly stand up and whip around to face him as fire shoots through me, and not just where he spanked. Still, I can't help but protest. "Hey!"

"You think you're going to strip tease me?" he asks. His eyes blaze.

"I'm not strip teasing. I'm tired and I want to go to bed," I say, bordering on a pout.

So much for his phone call, or whatever else he was doing. I've got his full and undivided attention.

My pulse races.

"We start now, Savannah," he says, spinning me around. I can still feel the stinging pulse of his palm across my ass.

I swallow.

"Start what?" I ask, not sure I want to hear the answer.

"We start practicing how you'll be submissive to me."

"Your... slave?" I ask.

Strong fingers grab my jaw as he stares into my eyes. "A real slave meets her master's needs without question. She lives to serve."

I swallow the lump in my throat and meet his eyes. I nod. "Yes?"

"Have you ever done anything like this before?"

I feel my eyes widen as I shake my head from side to side. My voice comes out in a tremulous whisper. "Do I look like someone who's ever done this before?"

"That's like asking if you look like someone who would lie or steal," he replies, still gripping my jaw. My skin tingles where he touches me. I tell myself to look away. I tell myself we're not playing games here. I'm only here for protection and I owe him nothing.

"What do you mean?"

"You can't tell by looking at someone what they'd do or what they wouldn't."

Can he tell by looking in my eyes that I'm not a virgin?

Can he tell by looking in my eyes that the only sex I've ever had was super shitty and was all about my selfish bastard of a boyfriend getting his? That I've never... actually... climaxed?

Does he know I devour romance books to ease my awkwardness and uncertainty around sex, because I don't want to come across as an inexperienced virgin?

Can he tell what I want him to do to me?

I lick my lips and swallow again.

"You're tired," he says. I'm not sure why his tone sends a shiver down my spine.

I nod wordlessly.

"You need sleep."

I nod again.

"So do you," I whisper.

"From now on, you let me worry about what you need, and I will give you what you do."

"That... I don't know..." I find myself at a loss for words. I shake my head.

"What is it?"

"If you do everything for me," I ask, as a touch of unease washes through me, "doesn't that make me like a child?" I shake my head, unsure of any of this.

"Not at all. You'll always have full autonomy. You can walk away at any moment." I can hear the implication in his tone. *But you won't want to.*

How much of this is "practice" and how much of this is because he wants to do this with me?

Can I trust Thayer?

He's the one Nicolette sent me to. He's my brother-in-law's brother...

Would Nicolette send me to Thayer if he can't be trusted?

Does she know what this place is?

We stand so close I can feel his breath on my skin. The raw, powerful masculine scent he wears makes me want to run my hands all along his hardened muscles and the flat, solid planes of his stomach.

I'm not sure that's allowed.

What would it take for him to allow it?

I'm not sure the word *allow* ever crossed my mind when it came to men, but with him... it's almost instinctual. I know before he tells me that permission and rules will play heavily into whatever it is we're going to do.

"For now, we need sleep," he says, still holding my gaze. Wordlessly, he traces his fingertip along the bridge of my nose, across the outline of my lips, down the length of my jaw. The places he touches feel electrified.

"Sleep," I repeat with a nod. The backs of my eyelids feel so heavy, I know I need sleep, but it's hard to reconcile my need to rest with the thrilling curiosity vibrating through my body. "Are you going to sleep, too?" I have this strange suspicion he's going to work while I sleep, or sit and watch me, and I don't know how I feel about that. The other reason I ask is because there's only one bed in this room.

"Yeah, baby," he says softly, his voice gritty with exhaustion. "I'm going to sleep, too. C'mere."

He curses harshly under his breath, almost as if he's angry.

I'm so tired, I can hardly hear him, but it sounds as if he says, "Why do you have to be so perfect?" I look down at myself, a little bemused.

Is that really what I heard? Perfect? *Me?*

Somehow, he's got the satin pajamas in his hands. Somehow, I end up in his lap as we sit on the edge of the bed. He pulls the shorts on slowly, the soft material gliding over my skin with ease. It's so comfortable it feels like the height of luxury. Next, the tank.

"Get under the covers," he orders. He folds the corner of the bed down as I climb in, my body craving the comfort and rest I need so badly. I sink gratefully onto the pillows, my eyes already closed. I sigh contentedly. This bed feels as if it were made for a queen.

I'm dimly aware of water running in the bathroom. Lights dimming. A rustle as he changes out of his clothes. The bed beside me sinking a little when he climbs in beside me.

So much has gone on today, I wonder if I'll have a hard time letting it all go, but when I feel the comforting warmth of his body next to mine, I find it easier than I thought.

The heavy weight of his arm strewn over my body. My back against his chest, he curls his strong body around me so I'm cocooned in his warmth and strength. I'm struck with the irony—the very night I resist having a bodyguard assigned to me, I end up taken into the custody of a man who will master me and guard me more intensely than any bodyguard ever would.

I like the warm feel of his skin against mine. I like the feel of his body next to mine. His strong length curls beside me, spooning me from behind.

My breathing begins to slow. The excitement he built earlier begins to ebb, still present but muted under the weight of sleep. He whispers something to me, but I can't hear him. I'm already halfway to sleep. Seconds later, I'm dead asleep.

I turn over in the middle of the night and press my body to his back, my arm over him. It feels right and natural to curl up against him, like we're born to sleep in the same bed. I listen for his heavy breathing while I'm falling back into sleep myself. Maybe he never fully sleeps. Maybe he's always on alert.

I wake the next morning long after the sun's risen. Thayer's still beside me. In the early morning hours, I turned back over, and he resumed his place at my back with his arms locking me in. Our legs are entwined. I blink, wondering if he's awake, when the hard length of his cock presses up against my ass and answers *that* question.

"Do guys get hard when they sleep?"

At first his only answer is a groan, before he nuzzles my hair and inhales.

Energized and rested, I'm feeling a bit more curious. I wriggle my ass against his crotch to see what he does.

He slams his hand against my ass. "Stop that." My clit throbs. Guess I got my answer, then. He wants me to obey, and my body likes punishment. This kind, anyway.

"That turns me on," I whisper.

There's a brief pause before he asks, "What does?"

"When you smack my ass."

"Of course it does," he half groans, half sighs. "Lie still, Savannah."

I obey and lie still. But I have questions. "So what are we supposed to do, not touch each other?"

He groans again.

"Why do you keep groaning?"

At first, he doesn't respond. When he does, he rolls me over so I can look at him. Oh, God, that was a mistake. If I thought I could control my urges before, it's impossible now.

Thayer is devastatingly handsome. Bare-chested, I get a full view of his sculpted body, all coiled power and honed muscle, from the breadth of his neck to his powerful shoulders. I reach out to touch him when I realize this is something I need to ask him.

"May I?" I whisper.

I watch his Adam's apple bob as he swallows, then nods.

My heart races as I reach a hand out to trace the stubble that lines his jaw. I cup his face just to feel the emanating heat, and the roughness of his whiskers. I run a thumb along the fullness of his lips.

"I'm guessing we're going to be here a while," I say, giving voice to the thoughts we're probably both having. "This won't be one night, will it?"

"I can't say for sure," he says quietly. "But if I were to guess, yeah. This will be a while."

I swallow. "So maybe we should get to know each other a bit more?"

Holding my gaze, he kisses my thumb. My pulse quickens even more. Next, I draw my hand down his neck to his shoulders, feeling the latent power and corded muscle. God, what it would be like to be beneath a man like him, to be overpowered and submitting to him.

"You asked why I keep groaning," he whispers, as I feel the velveted steel of his arms, his chest, his back, every perfect masculine inch of him.

"Because I want to do the right thing. I want to protect you. But you make it impossible."

I feel my lips turn down in a frown. I watch as his gaze traces the curve of my mouth. My hand rests on his back. I'm afraid to touch anywhere else.

"Why?" I ask. "I've done what you told me to."

I don't expect him to move as quickly as he does, but the next thing I know, I'm pinned beneath him. He captures my wrists and pins them to the bed as he fully demonstrates just exactly how much control he has over me.

"You don't know me, Savannah."

I release a breath. "Maybe I want to. Maybe you don't know me, either."

I watch his gaze darken before he shakes his head and whispers, "I want to destroy you."

That should scare me.

Then why does heat and need throb between my legs? "I want to ravage your body and hurt you. I want to lay you across my lap and spank you. I want to punish you until you cry, then kiss it all better and reward you by making you come for me."

Oh, *my*.

"Then why don't you?" I ask, before I can stop myself. Okay, that didn't come out the right way.

His deep chuckle unnerves me. There's something unhinged about it.

"My job is to *protect* you, Savannah."

"I'm not a child."

"You're definitely not a fucking child," he says with another one of his groans.

I wriggle my wrists and narrow my eyes. "Then maybe I have a say in this."

His eyes seem to pierce right through me. My heart beats faster. "You don't know what you're talking about." He shakes his head.

"Um, excuse me? Why don't I?" How does he know what I know and what I don't?

"Have you ever done anything kinky?"

I try to look away, but he grasps my chin and forces my gaze back to his.

I lick my lips. "No, but that doesn't mean I'm not curious," I respond. "I've only had lackluster sex, and it was so bad I regretted it." I swallow and lick my lips, watching as his eyes follow my tongue. Even pinned beneath him, overpowered like this, I feel sexy and in control. "I want to see. I don't want to hang out around here being the only kid not invited to the party."

"*Christ*," he curses. Then he nods, as if making up his mind. "So you have a fantasy in your head about what it's like? I'll show you what you want. But you'll see, Savannah." His eyes flash in warning. "It's nothing like your romance books make it out to be."

Well, that stings.

Jerk.

"How do you know I read romance?"

"It's no secret. We all know you read romance. Nicolette told us."

I will pay her back for this.

"Then what's it like?" I ask. "I want to know."

He studies me for long seconds as if deciding what to do with me. Finally, he shakes his head.

"I can't answer that. I have to show you. It can be scary and erotic, educational and calming, and pretty much anything you want it to be." Releasing me, he pushes out of bed. "Don't move." Shaking his head, he mutters, as if to himself, "I'm going to hell for this. I am so going to hell for this."

Why does that excite me?

His boxers are tented in front of him, showcasing a gloriously long and thick hard-on, but he doesn't seem bothered or embarrassed. My sex clenches.

"Stay there. Lace your fingers together behind your head."

Uh-oh.

I obey, shaking a little. I try to gain control over my thoughts, but I'm having a hard time doing that.

"If you were my slave, you'd serve me. But what may not be apparent, is that a master/slave relationship goes both ways."

I swallow. "How so?"

He shakes his head. "You'll have to see." A muscle ticks in his jaw as he shakes his head from side to side and curses under his breath. "Fuck it."

I want to reach my hand out to stroke his cheek, but he told me to keep my hands behind my head.

He walks around the room and opens a drawer, gathering things in his hand I can't see. The sun shines brightly outside our window, telling me it's well past early morning. I don't care about anything but what's happening next.

"Come here, Savannah."

I look over to see him pointing to the floor beside him with a... riding crop?

Oh.

My heartbeat accelerates. My mouth is dry. Somehow, despite my trembling knees and racing pulse, I make it over to him.

He sighs. "God, I knew you'd be perfect. Why'd you have to be?" He shakes his head. "Don't answer that."

Perfect?

He's thought of me before?

I can't think because the next thing I know, he's walking around me as if appraising me, tapping the crop against his leg. "You said that punishment arouses you."

I swallow, my mouth dry. "When you smacked my butt, it did. Not sure about *that* thing."

"Oh, these can be very erotic," he says. As if to show me, he places it over my shoulders, tracing each one, before dragging the little square of leather over my tank. My nipples harden, tenting the thin material.

"Did I give you permission to be aroused?" he asks, right before he snaps the crop against my nipple. A sharp flare of heat spasms through me, and I gasp.

"As if I have control over being aroused?" I ask, panting.

"You do. You'll do what I command."

Another sharp sting of the crop on my other nipple this time. Soon, he's flicking the leather over my shoulders and chest, over and over and over until my clit throbs with need. It's better than anything I've ever felt before. *How?*

"If you were mine..." His voice trails off, and this time when he says it, I imagine he's wondering what he would do to me sexually if I were his.

Ah, is that what he gets out of this, then?

I'm not yours.

Why does he keep bringing that up? Is it something he's thought about, then? Does he *want* me to be his?

"You would obey and know your place, and if I told you to do something, I'd expect it to be done.'

I nod. I think we've covered that.

"And if you didn't," he stands behind me, crop raised, "I would punish you."

This time he brings it down so hard I hiss in a breath. The stinging bite of the crop is more than I'm ready for. While my arousal seems to be heightening with every second that passes, the shocking pain of it makes me gasp in surprise. I'm startled by the sensations of pleasure and pain.

"Being a slave means service and obedience," he says. "But I wouldn't ask that of you. And I like more give and take in a relationship. Unlike other masters, I like my submissives to have a will of their own."

Unlike other masters…

His submissives? How many has he… been with?

I bite back a response because I'm not sure where he's going with this.

When he reaches for my hand and lifts me to my feet, I look into his eyes. "But I'm not your master," he whispers. "And you're not my slave, or even my submissive." The knuckles of his fist are wrapped so tightly around the crop, it looks as if it hurts. I wonder what's going on inside him that he continually does this push and pull, like he wants to flirt with me then regrets it, every time.

I nod. "I'm not," I whisper back. "But I'm willing to play a little."

His eyelids flutter closed for a brief second as if he's trying to regain his composure before he replies, "We'll have to, won't we?"

I lick my lips and nod. "I think so?"

He looks up at my hair, tangled since we took the wig off, and runs his fingers through it. I like when he touches me like that. Hell, I like any way he touches me.

"We have to cut your hair."

Of all the things he's said to me, this one stings the most. I swallow the lump in my throat. I love my hair.

"Can't I just wear a wig?"

"It's too risky," he replies, shaking his head. "It's much safer if we cut and dye your hair."

I look away, suddenly overcome with emotion. It isn't just the hair, but what it symbolizes.

"You okay?"

"I need a minute."

To my surprise, he pulls me to him. Tucking my head against his shoulder, he hugs me. "You're doing so well," he whispers in my ear. "This is hard, but you can do it."

I've never seen this side of Thayer. I hardly know whether to trust it. I nod against his chest and close my eyes.

Is he a different person when he's here? Is there something about my predicament that brings out his protective nature?

It's dangerous, I realize, as I breathe in the strong, clean scent of him, as I feel his heartbeat against my cheek and revel in the touch of his naked skin against mine.

I can't fall for him.

But how do I stop myself?

EIGHT

*T*HAYER

It takes all my self-control not to push her up against this wall and fuck her. Claim her. Master her.

We're in my playground, where I get whatever I want whenever I want it. She's completely at my mercy.

And she likes it.

When she looks afraid, like this is all too much, I can't stop myself from consoling her. Though Savannah's put up a brave front, I can tell she's scared.

It takes effort to ignore the raging hard-on I got just by sleeping with her beautiful body pressed up against mine.

I have to grind my teeth and force myself not to kiss her again.

When I hold her, I can feel how small and fragile she is, how easily I could crush her. When she fits into my arms like this, it's a vivid reminder of the vulnerability she likes to pretend she doesn't fight.

"Let's get this over with."

She draws in a long, deep breath, and squares her shoulders. Her jaw set, she turns to me with determination and heaves out a breath before she says, "Let's do this."

"If I cut your hair, you'll look like a badly shorn sheep," I say with a grimace.

Her eyes twinkle at me.

"You've got another option?"

I nod. "Have you met Cosette?"

"Nicolette's friend?"

"Yes. She went to school for cosmetology and is willing and able to help."

Savannah swallows. "Okay, but I don't know if I want Cosette to see me nearly naked in your suite."

My dick twitches. *Nearly naked in your suite.*

Jesus.

"You'll wear a robe. She'll join us after breakfast."

"Do you have room service here?"

"Of course."

She nods her head and bites her lip as I pick up my phone.

"Uh... Master?"

My lips quirk up. "Call me Thayer."

"Slaves can call their masters by their first name?"

"They can do whatever their master tells them, Savannah."

She looks abashed. "Okay then. Um. Thayer?"

"Yes?"

"How would we do the breakfast thing if I really was your slave?"

"I'd order you breakfast. Food that you like and food that serves you. I'd feed you myself."

"Huh. Food that serves me? What does that mean?"

"High-quality food that you enjoy."

"Ah, okay, so if I don't do dairy or something, you'd take that into account."

"Yes. We have a private chef who prepares food that our clients prefer or request."

She cocks her head to the side curiously. "What else do you have here?"

"Lots. I'll show you, since you're staying here indefinitely."

I tap Cosette's number. "But we have to make sure you're unrecognizable first. We'll start there."

Cosette answers on the first ring.

"Thayer?"

I quickly fill her in.

"Of course, I'll be there in an hour. Any requests?"

"Don't tell anyone where you're going or what you're doing."

Next, I order food while Savannah explores the room. I let her. The more she knows about where we are, the better. She opens closets and drawers and peers out a window. "Oh. Oh, my," she says when she finds a sensory deprivation hood on a shelf beside a pair of spreaders.

"Do you do butt plugs?"

I blink. "Do I *do* them?"

Though she flushes pink, she continues bravely, "I mean, like, do you use them? Are you into that jeweled plug thing?"

"Yes, of course. Not for *me,* but as my submissive, I'd require it of you."

When she turns away, I'm guessing it's because she doesn't want me to see the shocked expression on her face, but I'm not surprised. I have already discussed this kind of thing with her.

She's not going to be comfortable. I'm going to push her, and hard.

"Nipple clamps?" she asks.

"Do you have a mental checklist?"

Biting her lip, she thinks this over. "Yes."

"What else is on that list?"

"Um. Well, you've mentioned spanking but more as a threat than a kink. Is that like…"

"Both. Could be used as a punishment or for pleasure."

"Gotcha. And uh, what might that look like?"

I fold my arms over my chest and ignore the way my dick hardens. "Spanking you?"

She looks so flustered, it's adorable.

"Well, um, yes. Like… would that be over your lap? Over the bed? With your hand, or…"

Her voice trails off, or more accurately, sounds as if she's been choked.

"Yes."

"Yes?" she squeaks.

"It could be any or all of those. If you disobeyed me, depending on the infraction, I'd turn you over my knee wherever we were. I might take the time to get an implement, I might spank you with my bare hand. It depends on the infraction, where we are, what I wanted to do."

"Oh. I see."

I give her a pointed look. "It would be smart to obey me, Savannah."

"Right," she whispers. "Unless I, uh, wanted a spanking."

I nod. "Yes."

I love how curious she is.

"Do you use... other toys?"

"Lots."

"Oh. Well then. If I—"

A timid knock on the door interrupts her.

I open the door and take our tray of food. When I come back, she's gone.

"Savannah?"

God, this woman's gonna keep me on my toes. Where the hell did she go?

"Oh my God. There are like seventeen different kinds of body lotion in this bathroom!"

This is getting a little out of control. She's snooping in the cabinets. "Those are not all body lotion. Get your ass in here for breakfast."

"Alright, alright."

I draw in a deep breath. "Savannah."

"Yes?"

I stand with my hands on the back of the chair I pulled out for her and shake my head.

I need to get her into the right mindset, and immediately.

I sit down. "Come here." I point to my lap.

She flicks her eyes from my lap to my eyes, then back again. "Okay, alright," she says, walking over toward me before she sits tentatively on the edge of my knee. She's practically falling off, perched as if she's ready to fly. I grab her around the waist and yank her back, so she's nestled in securely.

"You're supposed to be my submissive. If you were my submissive, you wouldn't be afraid to touch me."

My hardened dick presses against her ass.

"Right," she says in a heated whisper before she wriggles her butt. "But I don't want to, uh, make things uncomfortable for you."

I release a labored breath.

This will be harder than I thought. *Fuck.*

"You let me worry about me."

I know what I can handle and what I can't. I set my jaw and reach for the knife and fork. She purses her lips and gives me a patronizing look. "If you say so. Is that how this works?"

They will never believe she's a submissive, much less a slave. She doesn't have to be that convincing but arguing with me could mean her life.

"Savannah." She flinches as if struck by the sound of my voice.

"What?"

"You are very close to getting your first punishment."

If the color on her cheeks didn't give her away, the husky sound of her voice would. "Is that supposed to deter me?"

I reach for her breasts and pinch both nipples, barely protected by the silky tank top.

"Ow! Thayer!"

I hold them between my fingers. "Behave yourself."

"Let me go. Oh God, that hurts." She squirms as I twist harder.

"What did I say?"

"Thayer!" She's trying to get out of my grip, but I won't let her go.

"I warned you, Savannah."

"Okay, okay, *alright!*" I let her go.

With a whimper, she strokes her breasts and massages her nipples, still squirming on my lap.

"Here," I say. "Let me." I push her hands to her lap. "Fold your hands."

Obediently, she does as she's told. I slide my hands under the tank and press my palms against her slender waist. Her breathing quickens at the feel of my hands on her bare skin. I take my time making my way to the fullness of her naked breasts, gliding my hands over her waist and to the warm, sensual space between her breasts. I reach for her nipples and massage them, taking care to make sure she enjoys the erotic pleasure.

"Holy *hell,*" she whispers.

I can't help leaning over and kissing her bare shoulder before I lick and nip the same place. I draw a moan of pleasure from her as I move my lips along the length of her neck, still massaging her breasts.

"That... feels... so... good," she says on a moan. "Oh, God, Thayer, if you keep that up, I think I'm going to—I could really just..."

"Climax? You would. You're so ready, baby, aren't you? Open your mouth now."

Warily, she obeys, giving me a curious look. Her lips part and her eyes are wide. She's so aroused she doesn't know what to do with herself. I slide a ripe grape between her lips and watch as she bites and swallows. Next, a sliced strawberry, followed by a tangerine slice. I continue to feed her small bites of fruit in between kisses.

She nibbles and swallows. Tilting her head to the side, she holds my gaze while she licks the juice off my fingers.

"*Fuck*," I grate as my dick lengthens painfully. "Can't fucking wait days. That's insanity."

I jerk my head toward the table. "Sit your ass up on that table."

Turning to face me, her eyes widen. "What are you gonna do?"

I press my thumb to her slit, covered in the satin pajama shorts. "I want to taste you," I tell her. She'll either be excited or afraid, maybe both.

I shove the tray to the side and hoist her up on the table.

"Thayer," she says with not a little bit of fear in her voice. "Do you mean you're going to... down there?"

Fuck me, how innocent is she?

I can already taste her, already feel her coming on my tongue.

"I don't know about this," she says, as I spread her legs apart and kneel in front of her. I arrange her legs over my shoulders and take a deep breath of the musky, seductive scent of her sex. I lean in and kiss her inner thigh.

"Relax. I'm gonna guess you've never done this before?"

"Me?" she squeaks. "Uh, *no*. I'm not a virgin," she says quickly, as if to alleviate any of my fears. "But I'm not... like *experienced*."

Fabien met Nicolette at a brothel we own. I'm not sure Savannah knows that. But one thing's for sure, she's nowhere near as experienced as her sister.

I want all of her. Her orgasms and pleasure. Her fantasies and firsts. I'll make her debut into the darker, kinkier side of sex unforgettable.

"You don't have to be experienced," I tell her right before I kiss her other leg. She's already damp with arousal, and I know if I part her panties, she'll be slick and wet. I stifle a groan.

I swallow hard, my mouth watering. Lean in. Press a firm kiss to the little damp strip of fabric covering her pussy.

"Ahhh!" Her hips buck, and I haven't even touched her bare skin yet.

My phone rings. I want to whip it against the wall and shatter it.

I press my tongue to her still-clothed slit and groan. She already tastes so good. My dick jerks in my boxers.

I close my eyes and inhale her scent.

"Thayer," she whispers.

I brace myself on her thighs and meet her eyes. "Relax, Savannah. Part your legs. And if you feel like you're on the verge of climax, you tell me."

"But I—" She bites her lip and grimaces.

"What?"

"I don't know what that feels like."

"What?"

"I don't know—what it feels like to climax," she finishes. "I know, I know, *lame.*"

I hold her gaze. "Stop talking about yourself like that, or you'll earn discipline. It's not lame. I'm just shocked that someone as beautiful as you has never climaxed before."

She shakes her head and looks sheepish. "I... well. No, I haven't, but it was like the worst possible sex you could imagine."

I don't know if I want her first time climaxing to be at my sex club on my tongue. Should I ease her in a bit more first?

"So you had sex with a guy that didn't have the fucking nerve to give you an orgasm?"

"I—well, he—yeah," she finally finishes with a sheepish look.

I give her a look that warns her not to start blaming herself again, or I absolutely will jerk her right over my knee, right this second.

"Fucking asshole," I mutter. I frown at her perfect thighs and gorgeous, satin-covered pussy.

She deserves perfection. She deserves a toe-curling orgasm—several, actually—that take her breath away.

"We have a lot to talk about," I tell her, holding her gaze. "But for now, I want you to take this." Punishment is only one way to teach a submissive how to behave. If I grant her pleasure, she'll want to please me, I know this. I've experienced this exact thing many times. "I'm going to show you how to come. I'll show you what it's like to have a man in every way you can."

I told her I'd destroy her.

My phone rings again. I'd silence it, but I can't when I'm here. I have to be on call for any emergency that happens.

Fucking hell.

I don't want her broken and hurt. I want her ruined for any other man after me. I want her for me and me alone.

I lean in and press my lips to her slit again. I savor the sound of her low hum of approval.

The phone finally goes to voicemail, and I take my place in front of her again. I go to drag my tongue along her slit again when she reaches her hands to my shoulders to anchor herself on me. "Thayer…"

I hold both her hands in mine while I kiss each thigh. First one, then the other. "Don't be afraid," I tell her. "You'll be okay." I chuckle darkly to myself. She'll be *more* than okay.

"I think if you do that again, it might be getting close…"

"This time, until you really know what it feels like, I'll allow you to come when you're ready."

I lean in and inhale her again. Press the tip of my tongue firmly to the edge of her panties and push it aside. She's panting when I—

A sharp knock sounds at the door.

Fuck.

"Go away," I mutter, my words muted.

Another knock.

"I'm going to fucking kill whoever that is."

Savannah quickly shoves her legs together. "I... can't just sit here."

"Go in the office," I tell her in a low voice. I don't know who I want to know she's here yet. I point to the doorway that leads to the office and yell over my shoulder, "Just a minute!"

I stand, cursing under my breath, and head to the door. I glance at the small screen beside the door that shows who's there without having to open it.

Fabien.

Why the fuck is he here? Doesn't he trust me? He was supposed to be traveling, goddammit.

I clench my fists. He knows Savannah's here, but he doesn't know I was just about to give her her first fucking *orgasm*.

I can see her hiding in the doorway to the office like a little snoop, trying to see who's here. "Go," I say in a heated breath. "It's Fabien."

With a little squeal, she runs.

I look down and realize I'm wearing nothing but boxers and an erection. Shit. I open the door just a crack.

"Where is she?" Fabien grates.

"With me."

"Where?" he insists.

"She's here. Where the fuck do you think she is?"

He lets out a labored breath. "I told you to keep her safe," he growls.

Who the hell does he think he is? I dropped everything in Paris to bring her here. "What do you think I've been doing? Why do you think she's here? Are you out of your mind?"

"She isn't safe if she's in your *private suite*," he continues.

I know exactly what he means. He knows who I am. What I like.

But he doesn't have the right to tell me to keep her safe then call the shots about how I do that.

"Nicolette will kill you if she finds out," he says in a rush. "She's sleeping since we turned straight around and came back. I told her I'd check on Savannah, and that I trusted you."

"Have you told her about any of this?"

"It was Nicolette's idea to come here."

He tries to push past me to come in, but I'll have to punch him if he sees her barely clothed, and if he thinks he can just waltz in here and take her from me like that—

"Get out."

Behind him, an alarm cuts into the quiet. *Shit.*

We only have two alarms here. The first is for fire safety, the second is one that the staff or a guest can pull. This isn't the fire alarm. Reasons for pulling the other alarm could be anything from a fight breaking out to a security breach such as an unauthorized person entering the building.

Fuck.

Fabien already has his phone out. He steps back into the hallway and makes a call.

"Do you know if they were doing alarm testing today?"

His brows are drawn together in an angry slash.

"No, we did it last week. I'll be right back."

I can almost feel his angry glare through the door when I shut it in his face.

Savannah's staring at me when I get back in the room. "What was that all about?"

I sigh. "Fabien and Nicolette are here."

Savannah grasps her robe and pulls it tighter around herself. "*What?*"

"Yeah, and they're not too happy that we're together like this."

Savannah bites her lip and looks around the room. "It isn't up to them, though, is it?"

A beat passes before I answer gruffly. "No. Of course not."

"Well, what did they expect you to do? Chain me up in an ivory tower?"

I walk past her to pull some sweats on. "I don't know what they expected, but it didn't involve me eating you out on my dining room table."

"Oh, *God*, when you say it that way—"

I'm starting to love the way her cheeks color pink.

"Yeah?"

"It sounds so dirty."

Savannah likes dirty talk.

I'll keep that in mind.

"There's an alarm I need to investigate. Fabien's on it, but he hasn't slept. Likely isn't much, but to be safe I have to be sure." Danger typically happens at night, when it's harder for someone to be seen.

"Got it."

"You'll stay here. It isn't safe for you to come out of this room. I'll be as quick as possible, but you can't risk exposure."

"I see." She eyes the door.

"Savannah." I try to put a world of warning into my tone, but she's unpredictable and headstrong and we haven't had enough time together yet for her to know when I mean it.

"Yes?" She gives me the most innocent stare. I growl, frustrated by my choices. I don't trust her.

Fuck it.

Maybe I should take her with me.

Or maybe I should chain her up in the dungeon and lock the goddamn door.

"I do not want you leaving this room."

"Mhm," she says, nodding. "You said that."

I also told her I would punish her if she left, and she's implied she might like that.

Fabien bangs on the door. "Thayer." He sounds pissed.

I point my finger at her. "If you leave this room, I promise you will *not* like the kind of punishment I give you."

She swallows and nods, looking all kinds of aroused.

I tug on my clothes. "Fuck it. Get dressed. You're coming with me."

NINE

Savannah

I pull on jeans and a sweatshirt so quickly, I almost trip and fall. I've been dying to check this place out during daylight. I know he doesn't want to take me, and I'm not going to do anything stupid and reckless, but if I'm here, with this once-in-a-lifetime opportunity, I'm going to take full advantage.

"Wig," Thayer says tightly, clearly unhappy about the fact that I'm going with him, and I haven't had my appointment with Cosette yet. He helps me tuck my hair under the wig, carefully securing every loose strand of pink.

I do a double take when I see myself in a full-length mirror in the corner of the room. I don't even recognize myself.

We walk to the door, but before he opens it, he stops short and spins me around to look at him. I start at the sound of an angry knock at the door, and Fabien's deep voice. "Thayer, get your ass out here."

"On my way," Thayer snaps. He grabs my chin and holds it tightly, making me look at him.

"We're investigating an alarm. Normally, we'd call in emergencies on secure devices, but occasionally we need to keep things discreet. I don't know what we're going to be met with. It's unlikely anyone after you has already discovered where you are, but our enemies have eyes in many places."

I swallow.

Our enemies.

How many do they have?

"I already told you I expect you to obey me. You do not talk to strangers. You do not leave my side. You hold my hand unless I tell you not to. This is not a time and place to ask questions, which I'm sure you'll have. I want every single person who sees us to believe that I am your master and you are my slave. Is that clear?"

I nod even though no, it isn't clear at all. I don't know enough about this sort of thing to pretend convincingly enough. I do know to follow his lead. I know not to do anything that will draw attention to myself, and maybe that's good enough for now.

Pursing his lips, he shakes his head. "We don't have time," he says with regret. "But we'll try this for now."

He takes something small and black out of his pocket and slides it around my neck. Without a word, he attaches a necklace to a little loop. Is that… a collar? I go to reach my fingers to it, but he smacks my hand.

"Hey!"

He growls. "No talking back to me."

Why did I think this was hot? He's driving me up a wall already, and we haven't even left the room.

He opens the door. Fabien looks from Thayer to me and narrows his eyes before he gives me a discreet nod. "You okay?" he asks in a low voice.

I look to Thayer for permission to speak to Fabien. Thayer nods. "Good girl."

"I am," I tell Fabien.

"Fucking hell." Fabien curses and looks away.

Methinks Fabien isn't a big fan of this whole sister-in-law as slave hoax.

"Why the alarm?" Thayer asks as we walk down the hallway that takes us to the main lobby.

"Suspected security breach by the dance floor." Fabien glances at me, then speaks in a low voice. "Maybe not the best idea to take her." I open my mouth to comment on there being a dance floor, but quickly snap it shut. I'm guessing the less I say, the better. Thayer curses and grits his teeth. If there's a security breach, we risk someone seeing me and, worse, identifying me.

Thayer looks from me to Fabien, then back again. "I'm putting you in one of the secure rooms. I won't be long. You do *not* leave."

I hide my disappointment, because I know he's right, and I don't want to do something dumb. But damn, I want to see this place. What if we leave, and I never come back? Nicolette and Fabien would be very happy if that happened.

"Have you given her a rundown of Le Luxe?" Fabien asks in a normal voice, as we walk toward the lobby.

"Some," Thayer says.

They're both picking up the thread that I'm here as his guest. I walk close to Thayer, trying to look as guest-like as possible.

"We have a strictly enforced code of conduct," he explains. "As well as a scrupulous screening process to ensure our members and guests are safe. There are secure entrances for members and guests, and private suites for high-profile members."

I nod, not sure if I should be talking or not at this juncture.

We arrive at the lobby, and now that I've had my blindfold removed, I can see everything. My heart races with excitement. This. Is. *Incredible*.

"*C'est magnifique*," I whisper.

Thayer inclines his head gratefully. "Merci."

Gleaming mirrors, sparkling chandeliers, shining marble floors beside plush carpets in front of the main desk. The water I heard last night is an actual waterfall lined with silver and white stones along a wall. Gorgeous chairs enrobed in matte white leather surround a grated, modern gaslit fireplace.

I am dying to know what the rest of this place looks like.

Several people give Thayer a wide berth as we walk through the lobby and head toward another hallway. I look above us to see a second floor above the first, wrapped with a balcony. I can't see much because Fabien and Thayer walk so quickly, everything passes by us in a blur. I wonder where they're going and what they're going to do.

It appears that this main floor is mostly outfitted for community. We pass the dance floor, then a spa. I see a few women and men in thick white robes sipping tea in a waiting room of sorts. Mirrored doors and hallways make it feel as if we're in a maze. I am dying to know what's behind those closed doors. Who goes here. What a private club like this really has to offer.

Out of the corner of my eye, I see a dimly lit room, another with velvet drapes that hit the floor, and a third with a half-open door, sunlight filtering in through slats in the shades. Thayer takes me to the last room at the end of the hall and guides me in. He looks as if he'd rather put me in a cage with lions than leave me alone.

"You'll stay here."

I look around. We're in a small, cozy, private library of sorts, complete with leather furniture and bookshelves lined with hardcover novels. Oooh, I could enjoy myself in here. "D'aw. I don't get the room with the velvet curtains?"

Fabien frowns, his lips turning downward. "This is not a game, Savannah." Ouch. I didn't expect Fabien to scold me, too. He turns to Thayer. "Let's go."

Thayer hangs back behind Fabien and lowers his voice. "You'll be safe in here. I won't be long." He pauses. "Don't test me, Savannah."

The door shuts behind him, leaving me with a pounding heart and enough curiosity that could kill not just the cat but the entire damn zoo.

I turn around and look the room over.

So maybe this isn't exactly a library. At first glance, that's what it looks like but now that I see details, I realize this is more of a... game room. From a quick scan, everything looks normal, like something you might find in a high-end resort. A pool table in one corner, table with a checkerboard in another. But normally, checkerboards don't have leather straps hanging from them, and pool tables definitely don't have stirrups.

Yikes.

The books along the wall feature titles I've never heard of before, but that catch my interest.

A Night with Master.

Power Play and Sexual Exploration

Subtle Mastery

Tied up and Taken

The Art of Submission

I pull out *A Night with Master* and look over my shoulder. Is this room recorded? I know this is one of the secure rooms, but does that mean it's private?

What would Thayer think?

I don't know why I care. He *runs* this place. What would be wrong about me reading a book in his library?

Against one wall there's a drink station of sorts—a small mini fridge with a glass door. Inside, there are little bottles of wine, shots, sparkling water, and other drinks I don't recognize. Next to the fridge, there's an espresso machine, mugs, and everything else one would need.

I make myself a cup of tea, take my book to the bench, and sit down to read. It feels proper enough.

But of course I can't focus.

I hear low voices in the hall outside the door. They pass, but I can't help but wonder who it is. A car pulls up outside the window and two people, whose faces I can't see, exit. They're accompanied by scary-looking tall men I assume are bodyguards. I wonder why Thayer put me in this room to keep me safe when it seems like such a central location.

I wish I could somehow explore this place without anyone realizing I'm here.

Wait.

Could I?

Thayer will be pissed. I know he will. I don't want to be stupid, but at the same time, I may never get this opportunity again.

I wonder how long he'll be.

Voices approach the door again. I listen, wondering if it's Thayer, but neither of the voices sound like him. They pause in front of the door. I know immediately that they're coming in. I look wildly around the room for a place to escape to or hide. I see a closet door and pray to the gods that it opens. I bolt to the door and grab the handle, relief washing through me when it turns. I yank it open and slide inside, pulling it closed behind me as the door to this room opens.

There's only one problem: this was not a closet door, but a door that leads to another room.

I wish I had my cell phone so I could text Thayer. If he comes back and finds me gone…

I stand by the door and listen, as I observe the room in front of me. It's another community room of sorts, this one apparently geared toward activities that aren't actually sexual or deviant.

Meditation pillows, yoga blocks, and a small table with tissues and a few small potted succulents sit in one nook. It looks cozy and welcoming, with ivory walls and calming music. Another side of the room houses a small library of books, modern, streamlined chairs that look comfortable, and another small section with canvas and paints.

I hear someone enter the room I just left. I need to find a place to hide, but when I hear their words, I can't move. I'm frozen in place, mesmerized.

"What do I expect from you, pet?"

There's a small cry. "That I show deference and humility, sir."

My cheeks flame. My pulse races. I'm having a hard time breathing.

"Mmm. What else?"

"That I follow your instructions without question."

I stand, transfixed, even as I know I shouldn't be here where just anyone can see me.

"This is an important lesson you need to heed. You must learn to control your temper because you know I hold you to a higher standard. And what happens when you speak out of turn?"

What happens? Oh my God, I need to know what happens.

This is a private conversation, though. I shouldn't be here, listening. It's wrong. And since I can't go back in that room, I should maybe... find Thayer.

If I act like I belong here, no one would notice me, I reason. I'll just sneak away—

"Hello?" The voice is behind me. My heart thumps madly.

I turn slowly, but whoever it is stands in the darkened corner of the room.

What the hell am I supposed to do?

As she steps into the dim light, I breathe in a sigh of relief. Tall and slender with long blonde hair that nearly hits her ass, Nicolette's friend Cosette looks at me with concern.

"Cosette." My voice is choked.

"Savannah?" she whispers. "Is that you?"

"Yes."

She looks to the left and right. "You aren't supposed to be in here. Thayer will lose his mind. This room is public with no security restriction."

I tell her quickly why I'm here. Her eyes widen. "Someone was in the playroom? That's locked until noon." She strokes her chin. "I'll have to tell Thayer about this. Are they still there?"

"Yes, but I don't know if you should—"

She opens the door. I cover my mouth with my hand and look for cover.

"No one's in here now," she says. "Come on. Are you sure you heard voices?"

I give her a look that tells her I did, in fact, hear voices, and not the kind in my head.

"Okay, okay," she says. "He wanted to keep you safe, and I know he'll be back here soon." She glances at a clock on the wall. "Your sister arrived this morning. Have you seen her yet?"

My heart squeezes. "No."

Cosette looks at me with concern. "I don't know why you're here," she says softly. "I don't know what's going on at all, but I know Nicolette's supposed to be traveling now. I just saw her by the dance floor." Her brow knits. "Are you safe?"

A lump rises in my throat. "That depends," I answer. "Is being with Thayer safe?"

Her eyes soften as she reaches for my hands to give me a little squeeze. "There's no safer place to be." My heart turns. "Listen, I have to go," she whispers. "I was supposed to be somewhere five minutes ago. But I know we have a haircut to take care of, so I'll see you soon."

She leaves after giving me another hand squeeze.

I want to see my sister.

I want to take what may be my only chance to see this place.

Thayer said he'd punish me, and not only do I not care anymore, I want to see what *that* looks like. Curiosity floods me at the thought of what he'll do if I disobey him and hell, I reason, he put me in this room that wasn't safe at all.

I look around the meditation room. Cosette said it was a public room, which I'm guessing means I should be able to access other rooms from here.

I'll move quickly and won't talk to anyone. I want to see my sister.

I open the door and look quickly down the hallway. I hear voices and see shadows of people in the distance, but no one is nearby.

The dance floor. Nicolette's by the dance floor, Cosette said. Thayer and Fabien were going there as well.

I walk as if I belong here, as if I know where I'm going and why. My heart beats with excitement as I start to take in more details.

This place looks *amazing*.

There's a room lined with mirrors, a workout area that leads to an enormous hot tub and steam room. As I walk past the spa-like accommodations, I see more and more, curiosity propelling me forward until I've nearly forgotten I came to find Nicolette.

"Savannah."

My heart leaps at the sound of my name. Thayer and Fabien stand nearby, both of them glaring at me. Thayer reaches for me. "Is there a reason why you're not where you should be?"

I swallow. "Several."

He takes me by the arm. My pulse spikes at the look on his face, and I know then that I've crossed a line.

"I told you not to test me," he warns.

Fabien purses his lips. "You could put her in my custody."

I blink. Uh, excuse me? What the hell does that mean? Being in Fabien's custody would be punitive, like I'm a child in need of protection.

"I don't need to be in anyone's *custody*." Ugh, the nerve!

He looks from me to Thayer. "I know how Thayer will keep you in line, and if your sister—"

"I'm an adult," I say through gritted teeth, suddenly angry that I've been tossed around like a stuffed doll and treated like I don't have the wherewithal to know what's good for me. "Thayer is doing a fine job of handling me, and what my sister thinks doesn't matter."

Fabien flinches as Nicolette's voice comes from behind me. "Savannah?"

I turn to face her. A few seconds ago, I didn't want anything to do with her. Now, my stomach clenches at the sight of her.

"Hey," I whisper.

"What are you doing here?" she says, looking around the room as if people with ski masks and guns are going to come and get me any minute.

I swallow. "I was looking for you."

She crosses the room to me in two steps and gathers me in a quick embrace. "Are you okay?"

My throat tightens and my eyes blur.

"Yeah," I whisper. "I'm fine. I'm okay. He said I was safe here."

"You are," she whispers back. "But there's been a security breach and we need to make sure no one finds out you're here. Has anyone seen you?"

I nod. "Cosette."

"Okay, go with Thayer now. Please, Savannah. Fabien and I will be leaving soon because we don't want anyone to suspect anything's amiss, and Fabien wants to investigate what happened to you. I know Thayer will keep you safe."

We pull away and she gives Thayer a piercing look. "Won't you, Thayer?"

"Of course I will," he snaps. "But she'll obey the fucking rules of the club, Nicolette."

Nicolette looks from me to Thayer. "She will."

"Hello," I say. "I'm right here."

"Go," Nicolette says. In my ear she whispers, "We have to hide you."

Thayer's hand grips my arm again.

I want to tell them I'm with him. I want to tell her she can trust me, that there's nothing to worry about. I want to tell her that I'm safe, and that Thayer's got my back, and he isn't going to steal my virtue or anything she's worried about like that, because he's a good man.

But I don't know if I believe any of that.

All I know is that if I'm not safe, how is Nicolette?

What if they recognize who I am and decide to come after her as well?

"Go," I tell her in a whisper. "I'm safe, babe. Go."

I look to Fabien and jerk my chin at him. "Keep her safe, too, okay?"

What are we getting into? Have we made a grave mistake associating with this family?

Nicolette swipes at her cheeks and swallows. "Stay in touch." She looks sharply at Thayer. "Make sure you let her stay in touch with me. None of this no contact bullshit, Thayer."

"Nicolette." Fabien's voice holds a warning I've never heard before. Thayer's well-respected here, and it's probably not too common for a woman like Nicolette to dress down Thayer.

What a strange, archaic world this is.

"I mean it, Fabien," she says.

Thayer towers beside me. I forget how tall he is when I'm not wearing heels. "She's safe with me, Nicolette. I promise."

She gives me a big bear of a hug before she lets me go and kisses my cheek.

He doesn't wait but tugs me to the door.

I realize with a sudden jolt of fear that if anyone saw us together, they might start wondering who I am and why I'm chatting with Nicolette in an obviously highly charged conversation.

I hate that I put her in this position.

When does she leave?

Can she visit me in Thayer's private room?

Where am I?

I have so many questions, I don't even know where to begin to sort through them all.

Thayer leads me to a small doorway I didn't see before. God, this place is amazing, and I want to explore every inch of it when I'm not in danger anymore. He slides a card along a little computerized rectangular thing. There's a flash and a beep and the door slides open. After we walk through it, it slides closed as quickly as it opened.

I realize then this is a security entrance of sorts, one they might use for discretion and anonymity. A place like this can't be cheap, and although it's well appointed, it's not huge. I wonder who comes here.

Politicians? Public figures? Other made men, like him?

I'm trying to take it all in, but we're walking at such a rapid pace through the club, it's hard. Everywhere I turn, there's something to see that sparks my imagination and curiosity: brushed metal, sleek screens, computerized panels lit with flashing lights. Everything around us is dark and sleek and modern.

I struggle to keep up with Thayer's rapid pace. Every few steps, we turn another corner, and another mesmerizing view captures my attention.

We arrive at a large, heavy door. Thayer presses his thumb to a scanner, and the door glides open. We're alone once more in a narrow hallway I recognize. We're almost back to his room. A wave of anticipation rolled with dread washes through me.

"You are in so much goddamn trouble," he says, his jaw clenched.

I swallow and don't reply, unsure of how I feel about this. I'm not sure this tingling in the pit of my stomach indicates only fear. My heart jolts, and I try to control the bewildering current that races through me.

Right now, all that matters is we get back to the safety of the room. I'll deal with whatever happens when we get there.

And then we're alone. In his room. The door shuts and locks behind us. I watch as he slides a deadbolt in place. Turning to face me, he removes his phone and silences it. He bites out one word that makes my pulse spike.

"Strip."

TEN

Savannah

"Now, Thayer," I begin pleadingly. Hoping for a little mercy, a little time.

Narrowing his eyes, he lowers his voice and repeats, "*Strip.*"

I slowly peel off my clothes, knowing that Thayer's about to punish me for disobeying him. I could argue my case, but I want to know what this is like. If the arousal I'm feeling right now is any indication, it might be one of the most erotic things I've ever done.

Still, I have to tell him what happened.

Standing before him in nothing but my panties and a bra, even the wig discarded in my pile of clothing, I feel a strange mix of fear and arousal and something that concerns me more than anything—the need for his approval.

Since when do I care about that?

I take a deep breath and tell him in a rush of words. "Listen, I told you, I was in the room waiting like you told me, and I heard voices. Someone came in the room, Thayer. They came and were talking, and I had to leave."

Thayer looks concerned about what I'm telling him. "Who was it?"

I can hear the hidden implication. *And why is he just hearing about this now?*

"I think it was one of your couples or something. That's what it sounded like anyway. I have no idea, but I knew no one else was supposed to be in that room. I figured it was someone you wouldn't want to see me, so you wouldn't want me in there with them."

He blows out a breath. "Tell me everything that happened."

I tell him everything I can remember—their voices, how many I heard, what they said. My cheeks flush when I repeat the words I can remember. My heartbeat thunders while I tell him all this. I don't want him to think I'm lying or embellishing anything, but it feels as if I were at a peep show in a private party, and I don't want him to know how those words made me feel.

He makes a quick phone call, I'm not sure to whom. They sound familiar and close, almost like he's talking to Fabien, but I know Fabien and Nicolette will be leaving soon. When he hangs up the phone, I have his complete and undivided attention, whether I want it or not.

It might have something to do with the fact that he looks both handsome and powerful. His eyes seem bright with anticipation. Butterflies flutter in my stomach.

"You know, if you were mine, I'd have to punish you," he says in a husky voice, as he begins to tug up his sleeves. He takes a step closer to me. I swallow hard and prepare myself for what comes next, whatever it is.

"Have to?" I challenge. He's visibly aroused, and very much not dreading what he's about to do.

"Have to. You're in my care. You stated as much to Fabien and Nicolette, didn't you?"

"Did I?"

"You're not going to sidetrack me, Savannah." I have a feeling a nuclear bomb wouldn't sidetrack him.

I bite my lip and nod. When I open my mouth to speak, I find it so dry I don't know what to say.

I'm so confused. Is he going to punish me, or does he only wish he could?

Why does the second option make me feel sad, like I'm bereft of something I'm longing for?

And why did he have me strip?

My pulse beats faster as he slowly, lazily drags his eyes down the length of my body. "I know why you left the room. I'm sorry you weren't as safe as I thought. There's been a security breach, and we suspect there's someone on the inside responsible. We aren't sure if it was accidental or not, and it will take some time to sort out."

I nod. Sure. Makes sense. That's what guys like him do. They "flush out security breaches" and whatever else that entails. I'm still pretty much fixated on this whole idea of punishment.

He brings his gaze to mine. The dark slash of his brows makes his eyes look as blue as a rain-kissed sky, and the way they're looking at me now...

"Have you ever been spanked, Savannah?"

I blink, trying to keep my calm, because I'm not sure why that question from him makes me all kinds of aroused. Seconds tick by that feel like minutes while he peruses every inch of me and clearly likes what he sees.

I shake my head. "No."

"Not even as a child?"

Again, I shake my head.

Slowly, he rolls up his other sleeve, bringing his eyes back to mine. "Have you thought about it?"

"Spanking?" I say in an oddly high-pitched voice.

"Mhm," he says as he takes a step closer to me. "Spanking."

I shake my head. It's a lie, though. I've been thinking about it nonstop since he brought up the subject.

Now that he's close, that masculine scent of his overwhelms me. Lowering his voice, he gives me another once-over that makes my skin feel on fire.

"Have you ever been dominated?"

I have to admit, I didn't really think of myself as inexperienced... until Thayer. Now I realize I've only been in one little corner of Planet Earth and there's an entire solar system of experiences I have yet to experience.

"So you're not a virgin," he says softly, stepping so close I can see the depths of his blue eyes. Each distinct eyelash. The masculine cut of his stubble-covered jaw and his full, pursed lips. The long, strong column of his neck and his dark hair that would be too long on anyone but him. I shake my head.

"Are you a kink virgin?"

I think my little squeak when I open my mouth to respond is answer enough for him.

"I see." He shakes his head and speaks in a low voice. "Why don't you tell me what would happen if you were mine, Savannah."

Why is it that this time, I'm filled with the inexplicable wish that I *was* his? Even though he'd punish me.

Okay, so this I think I know the answer to. "You'd punish me so I learn to be obedient." I nod my head, pleased at my response. I deserve a gold star for that one.

I realize with a quick thump of my heart that the way he nods in approval is even better than a gold star.

"Yes. Because not only does your behavior reflect on me as master of this club, but because you asked me to protect and watch over you. Since you're new, I would take it easy on you the first time."

I shiver at the implication: the next time, he'll be harsher.

Why does even *that* excite me?

"You went from one dangerous situation to another, only in this one, I have a lot more control over what happens." His tone sharpens. "You're only safe inasmuch as you follow my rules."

Okay, alright, we can go with this. I lick my dry lips.

"Right," I whisper. "And if I... were yours... that would be the wrong thing to do." I nod like a good little student.

"Exactly. I would put you over my lap. That's not always the way it would go."

Hoo-boy. Okay then.

Do I want to experience this, or not?

Yes, yes, so much yes.

I nod and shift my feet as I watch him pull out the desk chair. He folds his strong, sexy body into the chair, spreads his knees, and reaches for my hand. It feels so little and soft in his larger, rougher one.

"If you were mine, I'd lay you over my lap."

When he tugs my hand, I pull back. I brace my legs and stand stock-still.

I can't do this.

I tell myself to move my feet, to do what he says, but they seem to be made of lead. I try to lift one foot, then the other, but I can't move them at all. Suddenly, the thought of putting myself into that position doesn't sound sexy at all.

Then why is my pulse racing so crazily?

"I, uh, I'm not so sure about this," I begin. I want to remind him that I'm not actually his, but I'm not so sure I want to give voice to those thoughts.

"I wouldn't allow you to stall," he says sharply. "If you didn't lay yourself over my lap by the time I counted to ten, we'd begin with a visit to my closet."

Uh, what is that supposed to mean? *What?*

"Your closet?"

"Ten."

"Wait, what the heck is in your closet?"

Is this not hypothetical?

"Nine."

"Thayer!"

"Eight."

"Okay, okay." Do they all do this? Is this normal?

I stand next to his legs, feeling oddly small and out of place. "I don't know how to do this," I say in a rush of words, half begging him to take it easy on me. "I don't think I can. I'm afraid I'll do it wrong."

With a nod, he takes my hand. "Like this, Savannah. You'd lay over my lap like this. It can be hard to take that first step. Let me help you."

I find myself with my belly across his knees, my legs dangling. I'm not sure why, but I like the way this feels. There's a sort of warm reassurance over his lap, where I'm vulnerable and exposed. I tremble in anticipation, wondering what it really, truly would be like to be his.

When he rests his hand on my ass, a warm pulse of arousal spreads through me.

"If we were doing this for fun," he says softly, his hand running over the curve of my ass, "I'd make good and sure you were turned on first." I close my eyes when he encircles my waist and holds me closer to him, just before I feel the back of his hand on my thighs, spreading them. Heat flares across my face and chest when he strokes between my legs. "I might even let you keep your panties on before I made sure you were wet."

The first stroke of his touch makes me jolt, surprised with the intense flare of pleasure that electrifies my body.

Blood rushes in my ears at the first *slap* across my ass. It stings, but only a little. Warmth floods through me. "Thayer," I say, because I want him to stop, I'm so embarrassed and nervous.

He ignores me and continues, "We'd start nice and gentle, until you were thoroughly warmed up." A few light slaps show me what he means. Every spank stings, but only briefly as the bundle of nerves between my legs pulses. My mouth is dry, and I'm so damn aroused I feel like I'm going to combust.

"You'd know that I was the one in charge, but you'd also know you were safe."

Safe.

The word echoes through my mind like a mantra. I long to know it's true, that I really am, for the first time in my life, actually safe.

I feel the flat of his palm against my skin, the panties doing little to protect me. Ripples of pleasure pervade my senses.

I can't help but moan as he glides his hand lightly over my skin, and I find I'm trembling in anticipation every time he lifts his palm again. The intensity of it all makes my heart race, and I feel suddenly as if I'm going to cry. I'm not sure why.

I arch my back when he trails his fingers over my panties. My heart gallops.

Okay, so that didn't take too long for me to realize why people like this.

"But if this wasn't for fun, we'd have another kind of talk," he says sharply. My pulse spikes in warning a split second before he tugs my panties down my legs until they dangle from my ankles. "You'd be punished for disobeying me."

A flare of warning shoots through me.

Seconds later, he gathers my wrists in his hands and secures them at the small of my back. I open my mouth to gasp and feel the sudden inexplicable need to flee when he slams his palm against my ass. I open my mouth to protest in some way but find I can't breathe. He spanks me again, obviously quite experienced at this, as he holds me in such a way that it's absolutely impossible for me to get away.

I bend and squirm and try to escape, but there's no way I can possibly do that. "Thayer!" I gasp. My ass is on *fire*. This is nothing like I imagined, but I can't even think anymore because every time I open my mouth to breathe, I can't think about what I'm going to say.

I find myself tensing in anticipation now, as his palm slams down harder and faster, leaving a burning sensation in its wake. I squirm and try to wriggle off his lap, to escape the next strike, as smacks rain down and the spanking continues.

"If you were mine," he says through gritted teeth, "I would spank you until you fully submitted to me, until you begged me for forgiveness and promised never to do it again."

"I'm sorry!" I manage to say. A sense of surrender and remorse floods me.

I'm only aware of him stopping the punishment when I feel his hand come to rest at the small of my back. To my shock, I find my cheeks wet with tears as I release the tension I've held onto. I find I'm crying freely now as a flood of emotion sweeps through me.

My skin feels flaming hot and flushed as he gently runs his hand over my ass.

"There," he says. "Now you know. That's what I would do if you were mine." I try to stop my tears, but I find now that I've let them go, I have no power to stop them. All the fears I've buried surface—fear that I'd be captured by the murderers and tortured, killed needlessly like the lifeless officer who lay on the ground like discarded rubbish. Fear that I'd be abandoned by the only person who ever loved me, now that my sister's married and will start a family of her own. Fear that I'm not enough, that no number of degrees or accolades or praise will ever make me feel successful or adequate, that I'll forever be striving.

To prove myself worthy. To finally be safe. To find myself love.

"If you were mine," he says in a voice I hadn't heard from him yet, soft and gentle, "I'd hold you when we were done."

Wordlessly, he turns me over and lifts me. I'm a mess, but he doesn't seem to care as he tucks me against his shoulder and hands me a tissue.

"I would tell you to let it all out. I would tell you I know that must've been hard for you, but you're so strong."

A rush of emotions I can't quite separate floods me, as I let myself go and lean against the strong wall of his chest. I've wanted this for so long. I've been so lonely, so isolated. His arms wrap around me so that I'm completely engulfed, rendering escape impossible. Strength emanates from him. A comfort without strings or expectations, uncomplicated and reassuring.

Is this what it means to be vulnerable?

Is this what it means to be cherished?

Finally, I stop crying. When I hiccup, he reaches for my chin and makes me look at him.

"Feel better?"

I nod.

He bends and leans toward me.

"You can't kiss me now," I protest, horrified at the thought of him kissing me now with my tear-stained, reddened face.

"If you were mine," he says for the hundredth time, the vibration of his voice making me shiver, "you wouldn't tell me not to kiss you or touch you. Your body would belong to me, Savannah. I would do with it what I wanted and when I wanted. You would know you could trust me. That I would take care of you."

I nod. "It would be quite an experience being yours, wouldn't it?" I whisper.

I love the way his eyes crinkle at the edges when he gives me a rare smile. He doesn't answer me but leans in closer and brushes my lips with his. I want to protest. I want to tell him not to kiss me.

I want to tell him if he does, I might fall in love with him.

But I don't. I lift my face to his and welcome the kiss.

"If I were yours," I ask, as I lay my head on his chest, vividly aware of the tingling sensation in my belly at our nearness, the way he smells like masculinity personified, the warmth of his hardened erection pressed up against my ass, "would aftercare include making love?"

It wouldn't be just sex, but so much more.

"How do you know what aftercare is?"

"I told you. I've read the books."

"Fuck," he growls. "Yeah, baby. Aftercare would include sex."

It's all he needs. He frames my face between his hands and holds my gaze before he kisses me so fiercely, it takes my breath away. His tongue plunders my mouth, eliciting a moan as the tingling in my belly flares like a match to paper.

Somehow, he's made me vulnerable and made my senses more acute. Everything feels more vivid, more intense, more beautiful. He moves his hands to my hair and weaves his fingers at my scalp before he tugs my head back, little eruptions of pain along my scalp where he pulls my hair. When I moan at this, he grabs a fistful and pulls harder. A spasm of pleasure rips through me. I didn't know I could be so blissed-out by pain like this.

I reach my hands to his arms and drag them down the length of his muscled forearms as if to hold him back, but I'm holding on for dear life.

My world is brighter, vibrant and colorful, my senses sharpened and vivid while he takes me through a myriad of emotions.

My panties lay on the floor, forgotten. My red-hot ass scrapes against his crotch, but I somehow welcome the pleasure-pain of it all. He releases my mouth only so he can dip his head to my breasts. He tilts me back so my chest is bared to him, before he licks one of my hardened nipples. I squeal from the exquisite torture of pain and pleasure when he bites me before pulling my nipple between his teeth and suckling.

"You're a fucking goddess," he whispers, before he licks my nipple. "I've imagined what you'd look like naked and dominated."

No way. He's thought of me that way before?

"Have you imagined what it would be like to fuck me?" I ask him.

"Savannah," he warns, shaking his head. "Don't fucking tempt me."

"What are you going to do, spank me? You already did that," I say, leaning forward so I can kiss his collarbone. I love the way his Adam's apple bobs when he swallows, telling me that I'm affecting him. "Why do you have to be all stoic?"

"You know why."

I sigh and lean my head on his chest again. "Why don't you trust yourself, Thayer? Why do you hold yourself back? Yeah, I'm confident Nicolette and Fabien wouldn't approve, but last time I checked, I'm an adult. So it can't be that."

Instead of answering, he bends his mouth to my chest again and begins to lick and suckle my nipples. I forget what I was even thinking as my head drops backward and I surrender to the heated pulsing of my body under his command.

"Touch yourself," he whispers. "Touch yourself while I hold you and play with these fucking perfect nipples. I want to look into your eyes when you climax."

I'm still facing him, straddling him, while I obey. My hand shakes as I reach for my pussy while he stares into my eyes.

"Do exactly what I say," he orders.

I nod. I can't breathe as I hold my breath and start to stroke. My hips buck with the first wave of bliss, as he bends his mouth to my nipples again. I had no idea I was this turned on, but I'm already swollen and wet, so ready to come.

My need to climax builds as he licks my left nipple and squeezes the right. "That's it, babygirl," he whispers against my naked skin before he resumes suckling. I whimper and turn away, as if somehow that will help the growing need to come.

I cry out when I feel the bite of pain on my nipple. "Eyes on me," he growls. "You heard what I said to do."

With every ripple of pleasure, I feel so exposed I want to hide. I feel bared and open, but I want to please him. I want him to know I won't disobey him, not again.

But I'm not his, I think to myself, while he tortures my nipples and my body teems with pleasure and need.

He pulls his mouth off my nipple long enough to warn me, "If you take your eyes off of me, I won't let you climax."

I open my mouth to ask him how exactly he'll prevent me from making myself climax, but then think better of it. Something tells me he knows exactly how to do that, and at this point, I don't want to find out.

"You're beautiful," he says, holding my gaze. "I can't take my eyes off of you."

"Thank you," I whisper.

"Keep stroking, baby. I'll reward you for being a good girl."

I stroke and moan, my hips jerking of their own accord.

"When you're with me, Savannah, you enter my world. I'll teach you what it means to submit." He leans down and whispers against the curve of my ear, "Come, Savannah. I want to watch you while you climax."

At his words, I shatter. My body explodes into pure pleasure. I'm swept away in a tidal wave, enveloped in such a blissful sensation of euphoria, I lose total control over my body and slump against him.

"Good girl," he whispers as he holds me. "Good girl."

Now I know what Thayer meant when he said he would destroy me. He's ruined me for anyone else.

ELEVEN

Thayer

I want her so badly that I can hardly think. I can hardly breathe. I'm so damn obsessed with my need to really make Savannah mine, I'm driving myself insane.

I hold her against me after she climaxes, breathing through my own need to fuck her, so damn hard it hurts.

But I can't take advantage of her like that, and after everything she's been through, that's exactly what I'd be doing. She came to me for protection. I don't regret putting her over my lap and I definitely don't regret making her climax, but if I make love to her—

"Would aftercare include making love?"

Yeah, baby. With you, it absolutely would.

I love the way she feels against me, small and vulnerable and submissive. She clings to me like she needs me, and it's been so damn long since I've felt needed.

I know a part of her wondered if what we did was real or not, and that's my fault. I can't let go of the fact that we're not supposed to be together. Only a douche would take advantage of a girl who's barely legal and practically family, and I pride myself on not taking advantage of women. It can be hard sometimes, when women bring themselves to Le Luxe, ready to submit and eager to please, but I didn't earn my position by fucking them over.

Real? Goddamn. Nothing in my life has ever been *more* real.

I run my hand through her hair, willing my pulse to stop. To give her the aftercare and attention she craves. I hold her to my chest until her breathing slows and settles.

"I need you safe, Savannah," I tell her.

"I know."

I run my fingers through her hair. "If the people after you find you, they'll hurt you." I clench my jaw and tell her the truth. She can take it. "I'd have to kill them."

She doesn't respond but catches her breath before she finally whispers, "Really?"

"Of course."

"They call you The Savage, Thayer," she says softly. "Why?"

I grit my teeth. I'm not sure I want to tell her. Where did she hear that?

I just earned her trust, and don't want to do anything that jeopardizes it.

"I know who you are," she says softly. "I know who Fabien is. I'm not as ignorant as you all may think."

"I didn't think you were—"

There's a knock at the door. She looks at me with widened eyes before she looks down and realizes she's naked on my lap. My dick throbs and I stifle a groan. Hello, blue balls.

"Get dressed," I say in a low voice, as I guide her off my lap.

The sight of her running to get some clothes makes me stifle a second groan.

Jesus.

I rise, adjust myself, curse under my breath, and head to the door. I peek out. Cosette stands with a small black bag over her shoulder, biting her lip.

I blow out a breath. Totally forgot about the haircut.

"Just a minute." I look over my shoulder to see Savannah's wearing a little dress, likely with no panties on underneath in her haste to get covered. I close my eyes and take a deep breath.

"Is this okay?"

"Yeah, baby," I whisper tightly. "You look great. It's Cosette."

I open the door. "Hi," I say with a smile that probably looks threatening because I swear Cosette cowers. "Come in."

Savannah smiles warmly at her, looking as natural as can be, as if I didn't just spank her ass and make her climax on my lap. But when her eyes drop to Cosette's bag, her smile falters.

Poor girl doesn't want to cut her hair. Who could blame her? Someone with highlighter-pink hair's making a damn statement and changing that on her will mute her.

"Are you ready?" Cosette asks gently.

Savannah lifts her chin and nods. "I'm ready."

It's a big step, moving past her old self and into the new. A clear declaration that she isn't who she once was anymore.

"Okay, let's head to the bathroom. It'll be easier to clean up in there, and it's nice and spacious." She looks over her shoulder at me. "Sir, they told me to remind you your guests will be here at ten o'clock."

"Thank you."

I take out my phone as Cosette covers the toilet seat lid with a towel. Savannah sits, draws her shoulders back, and lets out a breath.

My guests. I know exactly who's behind this.

Me:

> Lyam, why the hell do I have guests coming here at ten? I didn't book anything. You have anything to do with this?

Lyam:

> Shit. I totally forgot. I meant to tell you I booked them.

Me:

> Who?

Lyam:

> New slaves to apply as willing servants.

I blow out a breath. Willing servants are women who consensually agree to frequent our club unattached. If chosen, they become available for single members of our clubs for hire. I knew he was behind this.

Me:

> Can you handle this, please?

Lyam:

> I can't, I won't be there until two.

Me:

> Fabien's gone. What about Mario?

Lyam:

> Needed back in the U.S.

Me:

> Gwen?

Lyam:

> Day off. Want me to reschedule?

Me:

> No. They're arriving soon. I'll do it. Thanks

I don't want to take Savannah with me to interview potential new hires, but I'm not comfortable leaving her unattended. I wasn't supposed to have any engagements this morning.

My phone buzzes with another text from Fabien, informing me that he and Nicolette have left and checking in on Savannah, then another message from someone at home asking about the security detail for Maman. I reply to an inquiry about our new building manager, and scan through a detailed update from our head of security. I'm so fixated on catching up on business I've neglected, I finally look up.

I blink and stare. Savannah's long hair pools on the floor around her like discarded ribbons. In front of me sits another woman.

I'd forgotten how Cosette's a magician with a pair of scissors. When Savannah turns to me, I'm transfixed with the soft pink of her cheeks, the perfection of her pursed lips, her bright eyes somehow enhanced by a shorter cut. "We'll need to dye it, sir," Cosette begins. "But the cut for now will make it easier for her to wear a wig. The dye job will take several hours. When should we begin?"

"Tonight. We'll have time then."

Savannah blinks in surprise. "We?"

"Of course. I'm not going to leave you to do this alone. I know it's a big change."

While Cosette puts away her things, Savannah's eyes are fixed on me. "Thank you."

I swallow and nod. Of course I can't leave her to do this alone, but I didn't know it meant so much to her.

Cosette stands, slings her bag over her shoulder, and smiles at me. "See you tonight, then?"

I nod. "Tonight. Thank you, Cosette."

As she walks to the exit, we follow her. "And one more thing."

Turning around to face me, she nods. "Yes?"

I keep my voice low. "I want to keep a low profile with Savannah. She's here for a reason, and I don't want to put her safety at risk."

"Of course, sir," Cosette says, inclining her head. "I understand."

"Thank you." I shut the door behind her.

"Do they all call you that?" I turn to see Savannah standing behind me, her arms crossed over her chest. I have no idea what she's talking about. She has little wisps of hair on her face and clothes. I reach over and brush it off her nose.

"Call me what?"

"*Sir*. Since when have you gone from Thayer to *Sir*?"

Is she jealous? She's totally jealous.

"I'm the owner of a kinky sex club, Savannah," I say in a low voice. "Yes, of course they call me Sir. Not only out of respect but because it's who I am here. Many of our clients don't even use their names. I don't demand it, though. Sometimes, Thayer works just as well."

I take her by the hand and lead her to the bathroom. "We have to go to a meeting shortly. You'll need to clean up and get your wig on before we go."

I wish she was mine. She wouldn't be showering by herself. I'd join her, wash her hair and body and choose her clothes. But she isn't mine, and she isn't ready for any of that yet.

So I let her go.

Nodding, she steps into the bathroom and grabs a towel. "I'll be ready quickly. Thayer?"

"Yes?"

She steps out of her clothes, giving me a quick glance at her absolutely perfect body, before stepping into the steaming shower.

"Have you and Cosette ever been a thing?"

I normally don't talk about my past or my relationships, but I feel she deserves to know the truth.

"No. I don't ever get personal with women who work for me."

She sticks her head out of the shower. "So that crosses me off the potential hire list, eh?"

I give her a withering look that for some reason makes her giggle before she goes back into the shower.

"Oh my God!"

I can't see her through the fogged glass of the shower door.

"What?"

I'm sliding the glass shower door open before she can respond. Hot water drenches me immediately.

"My hair!" she gasps. "It's so *short*! There's like nothing to lather!"

I breathe more easily, but it doesn't stop me from slapping her wet ass. I enjoy my red handprint on her naked skin.

"You scared me. Thought something was wrong."

"I scared you?" she says, clearly amused. "I didn't know I had that much power."

I blow out a breath and shake my head, sliding the door shut. "Finish up, Savannah."

You have way more power than you think.

I go back into the room and change because my clothes are sopping. I glance at the time. We have to move.

My phone buzzes with a call from our head of security.

"Yeah? Any luck?"

"No, sir. The coast is clear. I suspect it was falsely triggered."

We've been trying to find the source of our security breach with no luck. There was nothing out of place on the dance floor, and when we scanned our security footage, everything was as it should be. Then who triggered the alarm? Call me paranoid, but I've learned over the years to trust my gut instinct.

"Thank you."

I call Maman's bodyguard just to be safe. "Yes, sir?"

"How's everything there?"

"Fine, sir. All calm. Your mother went shopping with her sister today, and everything went as planned."

I hang up with him and text Fabien.

Me:

> You two still traveling?

His lack of response tells me he is traveling or something's wrong, so I text Nicolette next.

. . .

ME:

> How are you two?

Nicolette:

> Other than being totally freaked out at the thought of my sister alone with you, fine, thanks.

I smirk to myself. She's ballsy sometimes.

Me:

> You have a problem with that?

Nicolette:

> Oooooh, yeah. But she's an adult and so are you, so…

She sends an emoji with a zipper on a smiley face. I take a minute to think before I reply.

ME:

> Thanks. I promise she's safe with me. I'll take good care of her.

She hearts my text. I put my phone in my pocket.

What exactly does it mean to take care of someone like Savannah?

"Okay! I'm ready!"

I turn around to see Savannah in a tight-fighting black dress that looks like it's made of crepe paper. No fucking way is she wearing that.

"You are not going out in that."

"Young lady," she says, with her hand on her hip. "You forgot the young lady."

"Fine. You're not going out in that, young lady." I take a step toward her. She's a sassy piece of work and a ray of sunshine all at once.

Looking down, she sighs. "Why? I thought it would be appropriate in a club like this, no?"

"If you were available? Maybe. When you're with me? No way in hell, woman."

"When I'm with you?"

I pretend I don't see the longing in her eyes. I pretend I don't hear the yearning in her voice. I'd destroy this woman and won't let myself do that.

"You know you're with me because I promised your sister I'd protect you." I step away from her so I don't lift her in my arms and kiss the fuck out of her. "If I can't trust you to pick out something half decent, I'll do it myself."

Apparently, she's getting used to me because my acerbic tone doesn't even faze her. "Oooh, so we're playing that game now? Where you pick out my clothes?"

I close my eyes and exhale. This isn't a game. It never was. Does she have any idea what the stakes are?

I turn to face her. "*Savannah.*"

Paling, she puts on a brave front. "Yes?"

I blow out a breath. *Fuck it.*

We're going to interview new hires. She's with me for an indefinite period of time.

And Jesus, if I don't have this woman...

I clear my throat and point to the floor in front of me. When I speak, my voice comes out in a low growl. "Come here."

I love the way her cheeks flush. I love the way she holds my gaze as she walks over to me. I love how the energy between us crackles, like she's a live wire and I'm about to be burned.

When she reaches me, I pull her closer. I weave my fingers in her short, damp hair and admire its length. "Still perfect for pulling," I whisper. When I tug her hair, her eyelids flutter closed and she moans, low and deep and hungry.

I can't help brushing my lips across hers. She tastes so good, I want more. When she licks my tongue, I moan against her lips, unable to control myself. I lift her up by the ass, and her legs quickly encircle me. I deepen the kiss and claim her mouth, I bite her lip and revel in the sharp gasp of pain and the way she moans.

I've never wanted anyone so badly in my life. Every other woman before her is a wisp of imagination, nothing more than a fading dream whose plot lines I've forgotten. I already know making love to her would be fucking *unforgettable*.

I pull away with reluctance. "We have to go," I mumble with a growl.

"Where to? They can wait," she says, reaching for my collar.

"Savannah," I groan. "I have to do interviews."

"Fuck the interviews," she whispers in my ear, giving me one more kiss. I kiss her back, then release her, slide her onto the floor and give her a warning look.

"Don't tempt me, woman. I mean it. If you tempt me again—"

"You'll show me the closet?" she asks hopefully.

I narrow my eyes at her. "No, I'll tie you to my bed and bring you to the edge of climax and leave you there."

"Thayer!" she gasps. "You wouldn't!"

I give her a stern look. "I would. Happily." My imagination quickly darts down the dark alley of what orgasm denial would look like with her.

Fuck.

"Okay, alright," she says. "What do you want me to wear?"

I swallow and walk over to the wardrobe where I've instructed my staff to put clothes I picked out for her. I choose a slim-fitting pair of black jeans and a low-cut pale blue cashmere sweater.

"This is the softest thing I've ever felt," she says. "It's like wearing a cloud!"

My chest swells. I tug a lock of her hair. "You like it?"

"*Love* it."

Once she's dressed, I open a small black box I've kept on top of my dresser. "The final piece," I say, opening the box. My heart turns when I see the fine links of metal and the heart-shaped lock. I lift the collar and hold it up for her. "You'll wear things to indicate you're with me."

She watches silently, her lips slightly parted, as I slide the necklace around her. I lock it and slide the key into my pocket.

"I'm not sure how they'll know that I'm—"

I slide the second piece of the necklace out of my pocket and she eyes it warily. I snap the chain on her neck.

TWELVE

Savannah

I am going to be led through Le Luxe with a collar and chain around my neck.

A week ago, I'd have thought this was not only preposterous, but also insulting.

Now, I find myself more aroused by a piece of jewelry than I ever thought possible. Because it isn't the jewelry, I realize fairly quickly.

It's what it symbolizes.

I know he doesn't want to be a couple. I've gathered that much.

But it's actually not that he doesn't want to.

My gut says that something happened to him. He's afraid. He doesn't want to misstep or push me away. But I know that if he truly didn't want me here, he'd have gotten rid of me a long time ago. And I know that if I wanted to be his, my sister or Fabien's protests wouldn't sway me. I'm a grown woman and fully capable of making my own life choices.

Thayer commands this club. They call him *sir* and they obey his command. He's basically the commander in chief of Le Luxe, so I don't actually believe he doesn't want to overstep because he fears his brother's disapproval. That's out of character for him. Thayer apparently fears no one but himself.

For some reason, he doesn't trust himself with me, and I want to know why.

Now isn't the time for questions, though. Now's the time I pay attention to every damn detail I can because this is where shit gets real.

I'd been blindfolded and whisked through Le Luxe so quickly, I've barely gotten to see what it holds. Now, he's bringing me along as if I'm with him, and that makes all the difference in the world.

"You're shaking like a newborn kitten," he says as he fastens the length of chain on my collar.

"You're collaring me," I say, unable to hide my excitement. "That's a leash. This is where shit gets real and I'm so fucking excited."

He opens his mouth to say something, then thinks better of it. Instead, he leans in and kisses my cheek.

"You're beautiful," he says as he turns away, as if he doesn't expect a response. He says it like it's a fact, as if he doesn't tilt my entire world on its axis with every compliment he gives me.

I open my mouth to thank him, when a sharp shake of his head stops me. "No more talking without permission. We're going into the club, and you know what that means."

I nod. Risk. Exposure. Danger.

"I'll conduct these interviews as quickly as possible, then we come back here and have lunch while Cosette does her magic."

Since I'm not allowed to talk, I only nod again.

I wonder who he's interviewing. New dungeon masters? Security guards? Private chefs to make the fancy meals? Is this something Fabien would handle if he were here, or is it part of Thayer's job description?

He opens the door and steps outside with a look of determination on his face, like he's just entered into battle and he's putting me on the front line.

I notice right away the club during midday is nothing like the late night or early morning club. Guests filter in and out, notably different from the harried travel-worn families I've seen in most hotels. First, there are no children present at all, only couples—a man in a bespoke suit with a slight woman next to him, holding his hand. Two men in casual but tailored clothing, standing so close it looks like one wants to sit in the other's lap while standing.

Staff mills about wearing crisp uniforms and speaking in low voices, and far beyond the main lobby, someone in a black suit plays a baby grand piano. Rose petals float in the waterfall and pool in the lobby, and in the brighter light of day, I notice plush velvet couches, full vases of freshly cut pale pink peonies, and behind the glass door, a patio with a fire pit and a fountain.

I realize with a stab of pride that Thayer's the one in charge here, so he's the one who's chosen this upscale, luxury theme for his club. It is, after all, called Le Luxe, and for good reason.

Luxury.

While we don't move through the lobby unnoticed —I note nearly everyone at least glances our way— no one speaks to him. Whereas all show him deference, and respect as well. If Thayer wanted to introduce me, he would have.

This time, as we walk through the club, I note so much more than I did before. A part of me longs to be a member, to run my hands along the soft, buttery leather of the couches, to sip from one of the tall, fluted glasses of champagne staff offers on trays, to sit on the patio and read my book.

But I know what I really want. I know what I really *crave*. And when I see a man lean over and kiss the cheek of the woman beside him, his hand on her lower back as if to claim her in front of everyone, there's an unexpected lump in my throat.

I know I'm in danger. I know I'm not his. But damn, don't I wish this would all go away, and I could prove to him I might be the woman he wants.

We walk down a long hallway past the rooms we saw before. Now, however, more people mill about. I wonder if I'll see the couple I heard in the library earlier. Down another hall to a set of rooms that look like offices, he leads me to another room with an open door. "You did well," he says as he leans over and kisses my cheek. My chest swells at his praise. What's going on with me?

My skin flames when he touches me. He kindles me with the slightest effort. What would it feel like if he actually tried?

"Remember," he says in my ear. "No talking, please. I'll be as brief as possible."

I nod. We enter the room, and I feel myself immediately freeze.

This isn't a conference room.

It appears we're in the heart of the club that leads to private rooms. To the far right, there's a bar. With a quick glance, I note fine liquors and actual liquid aphrodisiacs. The room is immaculately clean, well-appointed with white and gray and silver accents, carpeted and luxurious, with the same velvety curtains and plush chairs I saw earlier.

But that's not what gives me pause.

The people who've arrived aren't... chefs, or masseuses, or anything like that. There are four of the sexiest, most well-dressed, attractive women I've ever seen. I don't swing that way and even I would want to hook up with these ladies.

"Ladies," Thayer says in greeting. "If you're here for the willing servant jobs, you've come to the right place. Here, we're in a community room our curated members frequent. As willing servants, we'd expect you to know your way around these rooms to perfection. You'll note a members-only bar with liquors and aphrodisiacs, comfortable furniture, and a small room behind us with bondage furniture and mirrored walls for the exhibitionists among us. We also have private rooms with dim lights and soundproofed walls, and themed rooms."

I try to swallow but find it difficult. I want to turn around and leave. Every single damn one of these women can't hide the way they look at Thayer, and I know exactly what they see.

Magnetic, sapphire blue eyes framed with dark lashes. Thick, dark hair I want to run my fingers through. The stern set of his firm jaw that speaks of dominance and strength. He's the perfect blend of arresting and sexy, charming and dangerous, what every woman craves and what every woman fears.

I find myself staring at him like they do, and realize my heart is pounding in my chest like a jackhammer.

"We'll discuss the positions available, and I'd like you to tell me why you want the job. But before you do, I'd like to explain a bit more about the position."

To my surprise, he pulls out a chair and nods for me to sit down without a word.

It's part of the act, I tell myself.

He needs them to believe we're a couple, that he's my Master and I'm his slave.

I fold myself into the chair and try to squelch my rising anger.

I fucking hate games.

I listen as he talks about the club, the rules, the expectations and pay. I find myself staring, my mouth agape, because I had no idea clubs like this existed and holy shit, they pay *that much?*

The truth is, though, I have mixed feelings about the fact that he owns Le Luxe. I barely listen to their responses as he interviews them because I find my mind reeling.

I don't like that he's talking to them about things like *obedience, service, and integrity.*

I don't like the breathy way the blonde flutters her eyelashes at him, or the way the redhead stares at me like I'm a beetle she wants to squash under her stiletto.

I don't like the way they look at him, and I don't like the way they look at *me*, with a strange mix of jealousy and curiosity.

I watch as he smiles at one woman and politely engages in conversation with another.

I watch in horror as he asks each one of them for an *audition.*

One at a time, they do what I long to do.

I'm shocked at my reaction when they kneel.

They demonstrate subservience and service.

They call him sir.

The redhead kneels in front of him, a look of adoration in her eyes. She's too familiar, too comfortable, and I don't trust her. When he gives her a rare smile and lays his hand on her head, I want to poke her eyes out. I look away, because I'm not used to this sudden temptation toward actual *violence* that floods me.

Soon, the interviews are over. He kept his word and kept things brief. By the time he tells the last woman to go, I've made up my mind. I don't like playing games with him. I don't enjoy feeling like I'm playacting anymore, and I'm going to tell him exactly that.

When he turns to me, I gather my courage, because it takes all I've got to stand up to a man like Thayer.

"Are we finished?" I say in a haughty tone, turning away from him.

"Yes," he says, staring at his phone. We're alone in the conference room. "Are you hungry?"

My stomach chooses that precise minute to growl at me. "No," I lie.

He looks up from his phone to quirk an eyebrow at me. "You haven't eaten much today."

"I don't need much food," I counter.

With pursed lips, he looks back down. "I'm ordering lunch. You need to eat."

"You can't tell me what to do."

The air is pregnant with the heat of his warning as he takes long moments to look back up at me. When he does, his gaze is dark and his jaw tight. "Excuse me? Do you want to repeat that?"

I hold his gaze even though I'm a little less brave than I was ten seconds ago.

"I said, you can't tell me what to do."

An electric current pulses through my veins at the narrow-eyed look he's giving me. It wasn't long ago I was pinned over his lap getting spanked, and it seems I haven't forgotten that.

Slowly, he puts his phone down and rises. I'm still sitting, so the effect is something else. He's taller than me by a lot when I'm standing, never mind sitting. Still, I will not cower. Not now. Not ever.

I lift my chin in the air as he stares me down.

My heart alternates between fluttering and thudding in my chest as I watch him walk to the door, his feet soundless on the carpeted floor. With one flick of his wrist, he locks it, then pulls out his phone and taps the screen.

"Lyam, are you back? Good. I'm done with the interviews and will send you my decision. I need some time to get some work in, and I'm asking everyone to leave me uninterrupted for the next few hours. Also, block off all access to the community room until further notice. Got it. Thanks."

He tosses his phone on an upholstered chair, then faces me with his hands anchored on his hips.

"Now that we've got my calendar cleared for the day, and before I deal with that attitude, tell me what's got you pissed off."

I look away, my eyes filled with sudden tears. I don't like lying and rarely do, but I don't want to tell him the truth. It means admitting I'm jealous. Why did I let my emotions get the better of me?

I start when I feel him near me, his movements soundless on the carpet. Strong fingers grasp my chin and turn my gaze toward him. "I expect you to look at me when I'm speaking to you."

I look into his eyes. I swallow, abashed. I can't hide this from him any longer. I clear my throat.

"You keep acting like I'm yours," I whisper. "You keep telling me what to do. But it isn't true. I'm not yours. This is only a game. It's only a role I'm playing because it's the way *you* think will keep me safe. But I..." My voice trails off because I'm not sure how to say what's on my mind. I haven't had time to organize my thoughts, and I don't want to say something I'll regret.

"Ahhh," he says softly. Do I notice a twinkle in his eye? Thayer's eyes don't *twinkle*. "I know what the problem is."

"What?" I snap.

Shaking his head, he sinks into one of the plush chairs and points to his lap. "Come here, Savannah."

"Why?" I ask, shaking my head. "I'm not yours. I'm only—"

His voice cuts like a whip. "Because I said so."

I remember the threat of his closet, but we aren't there now. I remember the threat of torturing me by not letting me come, but I can't imagine he'd do that *here*.

"And you'll punish me if I don't," I supply with mounting frustration. "Even though I'm not yours. Even though this isn't—"

The snap of his fingers makes me start. "*Now*."

I blink back tears as I walk over to him. I want to break through the wall that holds us apart. I want truth and honesty.

I want to be made vulnerable again. To know I'm safe.

I make my way over to him with more than a little hesitation. I don't want to blindly obey him. I want to know what's holding us back, and why.

So when I slide myself onto his lap, I cup his face in my hands. He might be the dominant, but that doesn't mean that I have no power.

"Why, Thayer?" I whisper. "Why do you hold yourself back? You're not afraid of Fabien. What *are* you afraid of?"

He looks intently into my eyes. He doesn't push me away.

"Are you jealous?" he asks curiously.

I won't lie to him. I nod. "Riddled with jealousy," I whisper. "I hated hearing them call you sir. I hated listening to them serve you. I'm not a violent person, and I wanted to poke their eyes out." I draw in a shuddering breath before I release it. "I know what I'm afraid of. I'm afraid I won't be good enough. And watching women like that audition for you didn't help my cause."

His hands cover mine. He slowly drags them from his face before he kisses each palm and places them on my lap.

I don't expect him to open up the way he does.

"My father died in a fire," he says.

I blink in surprise. I didn't expect him to respond to my question, and definitely not with something like this. While he talks, he strokes his thumb over the top of my hand.

"Many would say my father was not a good man. But he was loyal to his family and good to my mother and he raised me and my brothers to be fearless and resilient. He taught us that the measure of a man is not the rules he plays by but his adherence to the rules. He taught us to be hardworking, loyal, and fearless."

I listen, giving him space to tell me what he needs to.

"We were in a warehouse. I tried to get to him. I broke the windows with my bare hands and couldn't reach him. I watched as the roof collapsed, knowing he was gone."

"Thayer—"

He puts a finger to my lips. I kiss it and listen.

Oh, God. A lump rises in my throat and I swallow it down. This isn't my tragedy but his.

"I don't do commitments, Savannah. I don't do relationships."

It all makes sense. Why he owns a club where he's in charge but only dabbles in whatever it is he craves. Why he doesn't have a long-term relationship and likely never has. Why he pushes me away, only to draw me back to him.

He fears that if he loves someone, he will lose them.

My heart squeezes, as I feel my own fears begin to dissipate.

"It's not that I don't want this with you," he says, holding each of my hands in his.

It's that he wants it so badly and fears losing me.

I matter that much to him.

He's pushed me away from day one, but I know why now.

Some might say that admitting fear makes him weak. That he's less of a man. I don't see it that way, though, not at all. Thayer is honest and transparent. He demands the same from me and has the integrity to hold himself to even higher standards.

"I know why I'm here," I tell him. "But I'm not leaving. I'm not going to pretend that I don't want this... whatever *this* is."

Holding my hand in his, he kisses each fingertip, one by one. "You don't want to pretend."

I shake my head and whisper, "I don't. I've never been... into giving up control."

He nods. "I understand. Savannah, when a strong, capable, intelligent woman like you submits to a man like me, I feel like I'm on top of the world. It doesn't make you weak. It takes an act of great strength to submit. It means you trust me."

That's why he wants this. That's why he craves it. Though he fears losing someone he loves, he still wants to know he's trusted.

And God, I want to do that for him.

"Oh my God, this is amazing."

His eyes twinkle. Yup. They definitely twinkle.

"It all fits together like pieces to a puzzle. The yin to the yang!"

"Jesus, you're fucking adorable when you get excited," he mutters.

I give him a look. "Thayer, let me have my moment. I'm psychoanalyzing you. I'm an armchair—" I look down, "*lap* shrink."

"Savannah."

"All this time, I was thinking I just wasn't good enough, until these hot little hussies with those ridiculously huge boobs, which are implants by the way," I explain.

"Savannah," he repeats, sterner this time and hell do I love when he says my name, "hush now." I close my mouth. A feeling of calm washes over me when I realize how good it is to have him tell me something, to lean into that. It's why the command of his voice and his sternness make my heart throb in my chest. Because it's deeply, deeply erotic.

He pulls me close. *"Il n'y a nulle part je préférerais être qu'ici avec toi."*

My heart turns. *There is no place I'd rather be than right here with you.*

I run my hand along his jaw, feeling the rough stubble along my skin. I lean closer to him. His hands span the small of my back as he pulls me closer to him. I've gone through so many emotions just during this conversation, my heart feels as if it's going to explode.

Thayer Gerard, the sexiest, hottest man I know and master of this club... wants *me*.

THIRTEEN

Thayer

She was jealous.

Jealous of the women I'm hiring to work for me. They aren't even women I'd spend the night with, and yet she still let her jealousy get the best of her. It was the cutest damn thing I've ever seen.

She sees right through me. She breaks down every barrier I've ever put around me, intentionally or not. She tears down my defenses and bares me to her in ways I never knew possible.

I need to touch her, to feel her, to taste her.

I kiss her cheeks, her jaw, her neck, while she melts into my arms and moans. I kiss her throat, her collarbone, her shoulders. I kiss her until her head falls back and she's putty in my hands. I lean her back and hold her, then kiss the hardened buds of her nipples under her top, her soft skin, her soft, flat belly, and the curve of each hip. I press my mouth to the tops of her thighs, one at a time, until she's nearly panting, then I kiss her some more.

"Stand," I say in a husky voice as I lift her off my lap and stand her in front of me. "Get these off." I tug at her clothing as she does, though she moves more slowly than I do.

"Thayer," she says in a choked voice. "What if someone sees us?"

"I locked the door," I say, as I tug off her sweater.

"But other people have a way to open doors," she protests.

I stand her in front of me and meet her eyes. "Am I in charge here or not?"

She swallows and nods, her eyes a bit wider. "Yes."

I hold her chin firmly. "Do you trust me or not?"

A nod. "I do."

"Then take your clothes off before I punish you. And that *won't* be private. I'll take you to the room of mirrors and punish you as an example of what happens to bad little girls who don't do as they're told."

"You wouldn't," she says in a breathy whisper.

"I absolutely would." I groan. "Fucking hard just thinking about it."

Her clothes fall to the floor in rapid succession, one after the other. When she's standing in front of me naked, I reach for her and take a moment to run my hands over the curves of her shoulders, the swell of her hips. I commit every perfect, seductive inch of her skin to memory before I give her another command.

"Do you serve me, love?"

I can tell by the flush of her cheeks this excites her. "Yes, sir."

"Then undress me."

With gentle hands, she removes my clothes slowly and purposefully. Mine join hers. It's warm in here, spacious, and comfortable. I want to make love to her.

What she doesn't know yet is the structure of Le Luxe. While this room for community use is professionally cleaned and disinfected multiple times a day, it's the epicenter of multiple themed rooms, each with a different purpose.

I kiss each palm of her hands before I place them on my back. I rise with her wrapped around me, the warmth of her body and soft feel of her skin the most sensual thing in the world. I know where I'm taking her.

We kiss while we walk, gently and intently. I cup her ass in my hands and hers wrap around my neck. When we arrive at the door, I press my thumb to a small panel. It slides open.

When we walk into the room, I feel her stiffen.

"Thayer," she whispers.

"No one can see you, I promise."

"It doesn't feel that way..."

"It's not supposed to."

The Garden Room is made entirely of frosted one-way glass. Below my feet, we're suspended over flowers and greenery, a garden tapestry. Looking out behind her, we can see the blue of the sky and a hint of the mountains of Adjaccio.

There isn't a single bed in this room but one large, custom-made Tantra chair. Enrobed in buttery soft matte leather, the curve of the chair lends itself to a variety of different positions. I want our first time together to be memorable.

Wind howls outside the window, but it's warm and comfortable in here.

I walk us to the chair and sit, my legs straddling each side. The curve of the chair cups my back as I draw her down across my body.

"This is amazing," she breathes. "No one can see us, you're sure?"

I give her ass a little smack. "You heard me the first time. Are you questioning me?"

"No," she breathes. "No, sir."

I stare into her eyes. "I want to explore you. I want to show you what your body's capable of. But right now I want to make love to you, Savannah."

She nods. "I want that, too. So much."

Leaning in, she whispers soft words in my ear as I explore her body.

"You're so damn sexy, Thayer," she murmurs as I run my hands over her back, her ass, the soft, sweet spot where her ass meets her legs.

"Come here," I whisper as I hold her against me.

I reach into the small pocket on the side of the chair and remove a remote. With a click of a button, ivory candles in varying heights, arranged on a circular glass table in the corner of the room, begin to flicker. Another and the soft sound of a violin begins. The air, thick with anticipation, smells of fresh flowers. I've done everything I know to make this experience delight the senses.

The air sparks with electricity as we explore each other's bodies with our hands and mouths, kissing and licking, biting and suckling. I taste her nipples and she licks mine, I finger her pussy and she glides along my cock, she strokes my biceps and I nestle my hands in the small of her back.

"I want you in me," she whispers, her gaze fixed on mine.

"I don't want to rush things," I say, as I trail my hand down the length of her back. "I want to remember everything."

A corner of her lips twitches. "You don't have a video camera recording this somewhere?"

"Well," I tease her with a wink. I cup the back of her head and pull her mouth to mine. "No, baby. Not this time. But I can arrange that."

"Would you?" she asks in a husky whisper. "I would *love* that."

Her response sends a thrill through me. She's kinky as fuck and I'm here for it.

"Of course. You name it, Savannah. I want to hear your fantasies. I want to make them real."

I love the sound of her laugh as she looks at me and shakes her head. "I didn't even know I had as many fantasies as I do until you. You seem to sort of— spark the imagination, one might say."

"Funny," I say, as I play with her hair, my body heating with the press of her skin against mine, the sensation of the chair's low vibration intensifying every stroke of her fingers and touch of her lips. Accentuating the way she fits against me, molded to my body. "I was just thinking the same damn thing."

The curve of the chair folds her into me perfectly. Her legs over mine, her pussy lined up with my cock. I lift her hips as I glide through her hot, wet folds, and position her over me with a thrust. Her perfect cry of bliss makes me pulse inside her as her sex grips me. *Fuck.*

I groan in pleasure, moving her hips so she rides me. In this position, her nipples are so close, I can't help but lean over and lick them as I lift her up and down on my cock again. I'll remember her moan of ecstasy as long as I live.

Energy passes between us in currents, as our bodies become one. The slow, sensual pleasure between us builds with every second that passes. I whisper in her ear, and she whispers in mine. I tell her she's beautiful. She's an angel. I tell her how good she feels, how much I want her.

"You're mine," I whisper when her breathing hitches on the verge of a climax. "Mine," I repeat, when the first spasm of pleasure makes her shudder, and she throws her head back in ecstasy. "Mine," I say, as my powerful climax crests with hers.

I realize with sudden clarity the one thing I've tried to avoid has happened.

I love Savannah.

FOURTEEN

Savannah

I could sit here with Thayer, joined in this room and on this chair as we explore every damn position, until the sun sets and I'm half-starving to death with hunger. It feels so good, so right, to be with him like this. I've never wanted anything so much in my life. We tore down our barriers. We told each other how we felt. We told each other what we feared.

And we made love anyway.

"Savannah," he whispers. "Jesus, that was perfect."

I lean in and kiss his stubbled cheek. "I'm having a hard time reconciling something," I tell him with a teasing look.

"What's that?" He brushes his hand along the back of my head, smoothing out my hair.

"If sex can be *that good,* why the hell don't people have it more?"

I love the way he chuckles. "That's a very good question. Maybe they do?"

I'm sex-drunk so I don't feel like getting into the whole thing with stats and how many of my girlfriends think sex is overrated, so I only nod.

Sex is *not* overrated.

I lay my head on his chest. He sighs and holds me.

I close my eyes and commit this to memory.

Other people might see Thayer as rough and guarded, harsh and stern. I'm reminded of the way he tended to my wounds on his living room couch back in Paris. Sometimes, maybe those with the sternest exteriors have the softest hearts.

"Do we have to leave? I mean, there's got to be a shower nearby, and I'm sure you've got people who could bring things like our clothes, a laptop, some food, maybe our chargers..."

"Hmm. Those are some very good points," he says, clearly amused.

"We'd need some toiletries, you know. Like, I'm a bit intense about shaving my legs. Maybe some vitamins for stamina? And if I—oh. *Oh God.* Thayer!"

I sit up as alarm rings through me.

"What? What's wrong?" His brows clash together in concern.

"My birth control. I didn't take any birth control, Thayer. It's back in Paris, too, and it's been a few days now. Oh my *God,* what am I, a teenager? How? How could I forget it?"

"Savannah."

"Yes?"

"Relax. The chances of you getting pregnant are slim."

"But I don't want slim. I want *none.* Zero. Zilch. Nada!"

When he doesn't reply at first, I can't help but wonder what's on his mind.

"What? You look troubled or angry or serious about something."

He looks away and doesn't respond at first, but I press on. "Thayer, please, what is it?"

"We should've talked about this. I fucked up. I'm sorry, Savannah."

"Hey, buddy, this isn't on *you*. It's on both of us. We both fucked up. We had things we should've talked about but didn't, but in our defense—"

I wave my hand at this insane room of frosted glass.

"This is pretty hard to resist. One could easily get, let's say, swept up in the romance of it all."

Still, he clenches his jaw and lifts me off his lap. "It's no excuse."

And even though he makes a good point... even though I'm every bit as culpable as he is... even though I know I'm being irrational and maybe even silly, my mind begins to play tricks on me.

He doesn't really love you.

He wishes he had birth control because he doesn't want you to have his baby.

He regrets you.

My mind is sometimes a bitch.

Thayer, like everyone else in my life, maybe finds me too much. He owns this room, he's master of this club, and he has the sexiest, most perfectly experienced and submissive women at his beck and call. Who am I to think I'm special to him? Any one of those women would've thrown themselves at him.

I'm young and inexperienced. Maybe he deserves someone who could be what he really needs.

"Come here," he says, taking me by the hand, but he doesn't meet my eyes. "Let's get cleaned up."

I didn't see the door to the en suite bathroom, as it's sleek and hidden, flush against the wall like the entry to a spaceship. When he opens the door by pulling an embedded handle, I draw in a sharp breath. Though it's small—clearly only to be used for sex and the necessary cleaning up in the aftermath —it's adorable, and thankfully *not* bordered in frosted glass. No one wants to pee while staring at the pointy top of a pine tree.

An ivory claw-footed tub with a decanter of rose petals sits in the center of the room atop a hand-knotted silk rug. The marble floor is warm beneath my feet, and when I reach out a hand to stroke the shelf of fluffy white towels, I find those are heated, too. The shower's constructed of sleek chrome and glass with a large, square shower head, beside a vanity complete with glass decanters of cotton products, pumps with soaps and lotions, and small hand towels. The air smells like roses. Dimmed recessed lighting welcoming luxury and relaxation.

Thayer reaches for the handle on the tub when a low ringing sound vibrates in the other room. His phone? Thayer closes his eyes for the briefest moment before he curses under his breath. "I'll have to take that. I'll join you shortly." And just like that, he's gone.

Maybe we'll have to take a raincheck on that tub.

I wonder if this is what it will be like if I'm his. Will he always be on the lookout for the next danger? Will there always *be* danger? Maybe I've let myself romanticize what it would be like being with Thayer. Or maybe it's that constant self-doubt I battle, the fear that I'll be abandoned like everyone else in my life has done...

I dampen a washcloth to clean myself up and stare in the mirror in front of me. Rectangular with a frame accented in silver, it's well-lit and huge. I stare at my short hair and run my fingertips through it. God, it looks so different. Cute, and I like it, but it's... not me.

Not who I was, anyway. I don't know if I've made peace with this yet.

I look at my body, clearly marked by Thayer. My breasts are swollen and heavy. I turn and look at my ass, also very much bearing his mark.

Who am I?

I look at the tub and decide I'll take a bath in there some day, with rose petals and all. I help myself to the lotions and cleansers and freshen myself up, and a few minutes later, I leave.

Thayer's fully dressed and on the phone, immersed in a conversation in such rapid French I can hardly keep up. Again, I feel out of place, like a piece of a jigsaw puzzle that doesn't quite fit right. It's as if my being here has disrupted the whole natural order of things.

Thayer stares at the wall while he talks, shakes his head, and gestures, but when he turns to give me a half glance, he freezes mid-sentence.

"I'll call you back."

There's something in the way he looks at me that makes my heart leap into my throat. I'm not sure what it is, because it's foreign to me.

No one has ever looked at me like that before.

"Everything okay?" I ask, as I tug on my clothes.

He shakes his head. "No, but it will be." I don't miss the ominous tone of his voice. I swallow.

"Do you want to talk about it?"

A muscle twitches in his jaw. "No. I want to pretend that there's no danger, and that you're safe here with me."

A chill skates down my spine, and I give him a curious look. This isn't like him. Even though we've only been together, like this, for a very short time, we've known each other for a while. Thayer isn't the type to ignore reality.

"I'm not?"

In three steps, he's in front of me. When he reaches me, he grabs me by the elbows and yanks me to his chest. My heart beats rapidly. When I place my hand on his chest, I feel the rapid beating of his heart in time with mine.

"You'll never be safe with me, Savannah."

I don't reply. I'm not sure what to say, what he means. If I'm not safe with him, I'm not sure why Nicolette and Fabien arranged for me to come here, but I suspect he means something altogether different.

"What is it, Thayer? You can tell me."

When he draws in a breath and releases it slowly, I see the weight he carries and the heaviness that bogs him down. I can't imagine what it was like watching his father die, with his hands tied, knowing he couldn't do anything to save him.

Does he fear he'll lose me, too?

"They've found you out. I was afraid it would happen."

A chilling wash of terror floods me. "They found me?" I whisper.

He shakes his head. "No, not yet, but they know you're affiliated with us. Lyam's intercepted messages. It's no secret that Fabien's wife has a sister, and it was easy enough for them to track down your whereabouts." He blows out a breath. "We had a decoy sent back to America posing as you. She was shot and killed last night."

I blink, trying to process this. It's as if he's speaking a language I don't know.

"You had... a decoy... sent to America," I whisper.

He nods. "An actress who was supposed to divert their attention from you. It was a whim of Lyam's and he did it as an afterthought. We had no idea they had actually discovered your identity until we found her dead."

Someone is dead because of me. I know I had nothing to do with it and didn't even know she'd been hired, but I can't get it out of my mind.

Someone died because of me.

"Oh, God. Does Nicolette know?"

"Yes."

I cringe, knowing exactly how my sister will respond. She won't like this at all. Hell, *I* don't like it. I hate it.

"Who was it?" I ask, unable to forget that someone died pretending to be *me*.

"I don't know. I don't care. That's not the point."

"*I* care."

He gives me a little shake and gnashes his teeth together. "She knew what the job was. She knew the risks. She took them anyway."

Do I know what the job is? Do I know the risks?

It doesn't make me feel any better.

"So where does that leave us?" Will he send me away from here?

"That's a good question. Lyam's on his way, and we'll have a conference call with Fabien. We're heading into the main club area. You're going to see things you haven't seen before, and it's important that you take them in stride."

"Alright." I sound even less assured than I feel.

Someone knocks at the door. A minute later, Thayer lets Lyam in.

I stifle a scream.

Lyam's got a long, thick snake wrapped around his neck like a scarf.

"Relax, Savannah," Lyam says. "This is Princess. She's tame."

He strokes the long neck of the snake. I shudder when it flicks out its tongue.

"What are you doing with that thing wrapped around your neck?" I completely forgot he had snakes for pets.

He shrugs and grins. "I was cold."

"I can knit you an actual *scarf*," I mutter as he enters the room.

"You interviewed in here?" Lyam asks. I see his gaze catch on the open door to the second room. His brows rise. "You're my fucking idol, Thayer."

Thayer shrugs, scowling, and sits in a chair. He jerks his chin to a chair for Lyam to sit in, then gestures for me to come to him. Lyam looks curiously from me to Thayer, then back again. I can tell there are questions he wants to ask. I hope he doesn't ask them because I don't know the answers myself.

When I reach Thayer, he pulls me onto his lap. My cheeks flame while Lyam watches as Thayer whispers in my ear, "Even in front of my brothers, you belong to me. You'll do what I say and when. Is that clear?"

I wonder if this is part of the job, part of the scam, for me to masquerade as his slave and hide my identity. I wonder if he'll still be like this when the people after me are no longer a threat.

I wonder if I want him to.

I gasp when he grips my leg. "Answer me."

I nod. "Yes. Yessir!"

Lyam doesn't even look at us.

So this is normal for them, then. My whole body warms against Thayer's, as he wraps his arms around me like he's buckling me into a seat, only the seat is *him*. I shiver when he puts his mouth to my ear. "Very good, Savannah. You passed the test."

Without explanation, he pulls out a laptop and hits the power button. Fabien and Nicolette sit on the screen in front of us, and here I am *sitting in Thayer's lap*.

There's no turning back. Even if this was part of the act, there's no reason for him to have me sitting on his lap when no one else is here, and no one else can see me. I know then that Thayer's making an emphatic declaration for his brothers to see: we're together.

Fabien's gaze darkens, and Nicolette looks as if she wants to reach through the screen and smack Thayer. I'm suddenly glad it's hard to make eye contact on a conference call.

I swallow hard and lace my fingers in Thayer's.

Nicolette pulls herself together and gives me a little wave. I give her a little wave back.

Phew.

I want to reach out into the screen and hug her. I want her to tell me it's okay, that no one else is going to die because of me... including *me*.

I want her to tell me what it's like being in love with a mobster.

Fabien clears his throat. "Savannah, how are you?"

"Other than being nearly smothered by your very overprotective brother? I'm peachy."

Nicolette smiles and actually laughs. "Tell me about it." She turns to Thayer. "Thayer, are you taking advantage of my little sister?"

Oh, yeah, my sister and I have a lot to talk about.

"Taking advantage?" he asks in that voice that I immediately know means business. "What do you mean?"

I sit up straighter, even though I'm on his lap. "No one's taking advantage of anyone, Nicolette, and you and I have a lot of catching up to do."

Nicolette blinks. Lyam laughs out loud, and Fabien clears his throat. "Tell us what happened, Lyam. Fill us in."

Lyam straightens in his seat. "Nicolette, Savannah, you're family now. No reason to hide anything." He strokes his damn snake. She practically purrs.

I sit still, listening and hoping that the damn thing can't reach me.

"First, I want to know how much you two know."

Nicolette's eyes widen. "About what?"

"Who we are. What we do."

Nicolette looks at Fabien. He shrugs. "Go on."

Nicolette smiles. "You guys are a badass crime ring. No one fucks with you. You're friends with the Rossis. You help their Italian wine business as a front, and God knows what you do behind the scenes. Fabien's like the C.E.O., Thayer's the scary one who kicks ass, and Lyam's the smart one who knows all about operations and computers and shit like that."

Lyam's eyebrows rise. "That's a little more than I thought you'd know." He turns to me. "You follow?"

I nod. "Of course."

"I have networks I run. Servers," Lyam continues. "I've got spies and accomplices from here to the States, throughout Southern Asia, and in multiple cities throughout the world. If I want to flag someone or something, it's done. So as soon as you became an eyewitness, I put out feelers. Someone saw you. That someone asked around, looking for answers. Your waitress at a nearby restaurant pulled your tab, where you signed your real name and used a credit card tied to your real address."

Fabien curses.

"It was only a matter of time," Thayer says placidly. I look at him in surprise. His grip tightens on me. "We knew they'd find her. She's too difficult to hide. She doesn't blend in like other girls."

He runs his hand down the length of my thigh, out of the sight of the others.

"You act like you expected this," Nicolette says, her tone hard.

"I did," Thayer responds. "Why do you think I brought her to a place where I was most feared?"

The Savage. They call him The Savage.

My heart beats rapidly.

It's time I found out why.

"Where you've got the most control," Lyam says as if he understands this perfectly. "Of course. So rumor has it she's been traced back to us."

What has he done?

"Is Maman safe?" Fabien asks.

"Yes." Thayer's voice rumbles behind me. "I've had her moved and tripled her guard. No one will touch her."

I feel the wall of his chest at my back, the tightness of his arms around me. Thayer's a fortress no matter the threat.

"It looks like they circled Paris first, but the second trip, they took Cousin Milo with them. They interrogated and beat him and dropped him back on our doorstep. He won't tell me what he's confessed."

Oh my God. One person dead, another in hiding, and a third beaten because of me? Where will this stop?

Fabien nods. "I'm not worried. They took him because he's an easy target, but even he doesn't know where you are. We've done well not to disclose the information on your whereabouts."

Thayer nods. "Only members know about us."

I turn to them. "What about the new hires, though? Were they all members?"

Lyam nods. "Yes."

The doubts I had before resurface now that I know those women, the ones who applied for the job of *willing servants,* are already members here.

"Well, how do you know that the members don't talk, though?" I mean, that part seems obvious, I would think.

"They sign nondisclosure agreements when they join," Thayer says. "And failure to abide by the agreement brings..." he pauses. "Serious consequences."

So they rely on the Gerard family name to ensure safety and anonymity. I make the logical conclusion that fear of Thayer has a lot to do with this.

"There's no real way of being completely bulletproof." His grip tightens, and I feel the hidden implication. *Which is why I'm here.*

"Get Milo on the phone," Thayer says.

"No need." Lyam clears his throat. "I had him brought here."

Thayer gently puts me on the floor in front of him. "I'm going to have a talk with him."

"Thayer," Fabien says in a warning tone. "Don't overdo it."

Thayer shrugs. "Of course not."

Even Lyam's on his feet. "Thayer, for real, man—"

"I said I won't overdo it," Thayer replies. "Now you two do your fucking jobs. My sources say they went after our old stomping grounds. They found no one there but they asked around. Likely knew that we'd relocate."

"Did anyone tell them anything?"

"We don't know. Savannah, you'll come with me."

Nicolette pales. "Thayer, you can't take her with you. Not if you're going to—if you're—"

"I've got this, Nicolette." Thayer's voice is like ice. I stare at him and then my sister on the screen. "She'll be safe."

Nicolette cringes and looks at Fabien, who gives her an impassive look.

Oh, lovely.

"Can I have a word with my sister?" I ask.

Thayer growls but nods. "Yes, of course. Take it in there." He jerks his chin to the glass-paneled room.

"Thank you," I whisper. I take the tablet with me.

"Hey," I say warmly to her after I close the door.

She looks at me with concern. "You okay?"

"Of course. I'm fine. I just wanted to talk to you about something."

"What's that?"

I look over my shoulder and head to the bathroom. I sit on the side of the huge tub and cross my arms. "Can you... tell me..." I look over my shoulder and listen. Thayer's in deep conversation with Lyam and neither are paying any attention to me. On the other side of the tablet, Fabien's left the room. "Why do they call him *Le Sauvage*?" I whisper.

"I'll tell you what I know if you answer *me* an honest question," she retorts. I grumble but nod.

"Okay, fine."

Please don't ask me about sex, please don't ask me about sex.

"Are you two a couple? Or are you... keeping things just... friendly?" She squirms uncomfortably. Then we'll get right down to it.

"Couple. Anything else?"

Nicolette's eyes widen. "Oh, God. Are you serious?"

"Nicolette," I say seriously. "Listen, we don't have time to talk about this, but I just want to remind you I'm an adult, okay?"

Cringing, she blows out a breath. "Okay. Alright, yes, yes, I know, you're an adult. And I love Thayer like a brother, it's just that—well, like you said. They call him The Savage."

I look over my shoulder to see if he's there, but it looks as if he's given us privacy. I ask her in a rush of words, "Tell me what you know."

She bites her lip. "Okay, alright, so... lemme think. Well, they say he's the first to show loyalty and bravery in a showdown. Like he will take the side of whoever's cause he supports no matter the consequences."

So that sounds commendable, not *damnable*.

She continues. "He's been known to outwit police officers in a high-speed chase. He drives like a damn demon."

I nod. Haven't seen him drive yet but I've seen the demon-thing alright.

But none of those things are *savage*.

She speaks in a hushed whisper all in a rush, trying to tell me quickly.

"He once firebombed an enemy's private property. The crime? Sex trafficking."

Almost heroic, if you ask me—

Her voice gets even quieter. "He'll ruthlessly punish

people he thinks deserve it."

My belly clenches. You don't say?

"He once... tortured someone to death and left him tied to a flagpole outside an enemy hideout as a warning. The guy he punished was a rapist."

Now we're getting into some savagery.

"He drowned an early recruit who betrayed his family in the Seine. And once, when someone came into Le Luxe without permission, with the apparent intent to harm one of his girls? He violently interrogated him. I didn't see it, but I... heard it." She shudders.

I have to ignore the surge of jealousy at the phrase *one of his girls,* but it almost makes me gloss over the whole *violently interrogated* thing.

"You forgot throwing the trafficker off the roof," says a deep, not very amused voice, behind me. "I've also kidnapped various people for ransom, and once set a car on fire when the motherfucker who double-crossed my mother was still inside. Hmm. What am I forgetting?"

Nicolette squeals. "She asked, Thayer, and you be nice to her!"

Thayer shakes his head. "Jesus, Nicolette. I've had enough of this." He crosses the room to me and shuts off the tablet. "Conversation over." He tosses the tablet across the room. It crashes against the wall and shatters.

"Thayer!"

I stare at him, not sure what to say. My heart beats so fast I feel faint.

Without a word, he grabs my hand and yanks me to the other room. Lyam's gone.

I'm alone with the man called The Savage.

FIFTEEN

Savannah

This time, I don't take in every beautiful, elegant, stunning detail of the club.

This time, I only notice the way the people here look at him.

When we walk through Le Luxe with my hand in his—not held like a lover's stroll or two companions, but like prison cuffs on an inmate—they give him wide berth.

Where my word is law and my command absolute.

Uniformed staff quietly fades into the periphery like Thayer's made of fire and they don't want to be scorched. I note every set of wide eyes, the whispered voices, the way they slip out of the way and carefully leave his path.

I remember the way his mother told me she can't control him, that he doesn't listen to her. I've heard the way Fabien treats him with kid gloves, like he's a bomb about to detonate. I've even seen fearless, ballsy Lyam retreat and give him space when he needs it.

Like... now.

And here I am, hidden in a club that may as well be his lair, falling for a man who's tortured, maimed, and killed people in the name of loyalty and justice. Everyone with half a brain fears him, and yet I've jumped into the man's *bed*.

"Thayer."

"Be quiet."

I clamp my lips shut because I'm thinking this might not be the best time to pick a battle.

Large men, clearly bodyguards capable of inflicting some serious damage, step aside to let us pass. He holds the chain to my collar in his hand. I half forgot about that but remember it vividly when a quick tug tightens the metal at my neck.

The crowds part and hide like they're running to take cover from an impending volcanic eruption.

And finally, we're alone.

I don't know what to expect from him. He's a savage and he's ruthless, but hell if that doesn't make me want him even more. I don't know why my brain behaves the way it does, but I can't seem to stop myself.

I want more of him. With every frown, my heart beats faster. With every searing glance, I crave his touch. Thayer Gerard is a tornado, but I know—I'm safe within the eye of the storm.

Or am I?

He opens the door to his room without a word and brings me inside. I stand. My feet planted on either side of me, waiting, while he locks the door and turns to face me.

"I didn't mean—"

But I did mean. I'm not going to lie. I shake my head and rephrase.

"I wanted to know."

Thayer breathes heavily, like a dragon about to blast his fiery breath and burn down full cities. "I know."

I pause, unsure of how to respond.

"Then why didn't you ask *me*?" he asks, genuine curiosity in his tone. "I would've told you everything."

I swallow, unsure of how to proceed. "I wanted to talk to my sister. I wanted her opinion."

He cocks his head at me. "Is that how you make your decisions, Savannah? By committee?"

Ouch.

"There's a difference between asking my trusted sister who's practically my guardian for her opinion and asking a *committee*."

"Is there?"

I scowl right back at him, determined to make my point. "Of course there is. My sister and Fabien expressed concern about me being taken into your care and I wanted to know why."

He takes a step closer to me and grabs my chin, not harshly, but not gently.

"Did you?"

I swallow. "I did."

"You knew why. You've seen who I am. You know what I like. Your questions have nothing to do with me and everything to do with *you*."

What?

He runs his hands down the length of my body and when he reaches my ass, he squeezes, hard. "Your heart races when I overpower you. You climax so hard you're breathless when I make you come. You crave being dominated and controlled, but you can't rationalize why. What we have here is everything those out there will tell you is wrong, yet you can't turn away."

I blink, staring at him because it's all true, every word.

"I've shown you your dark side and it scares you. And you know that you can't turn away now."

Without warning, his mouth clashes against mine so roughly I moan, our tongues tangled in a brief but breathtaking, savage kiss. He pulls away, panting. "And neither can I."

He's right. Oh, God, he's right. I know that everything he says is true, and I know how badly I crave this. If he left me right now, I'd feel bereft. I'd always wonder what could have been. I'd be disappointed in anything less than *this,* than *us.*

"You want to know what I've done? Does that matter to you?"

Does it? Does it make him who he is today?

"I don't regret a single damn thing I've done," he says, and grabs my waist, unsnapping and unzipping to disrobe me. Next, the sweater, tugged over my head to join the small pile of clothes on the floor. "I don't let anyone or anything come between justice and the people I love. I show mercy to no one."

I breathe heavily, my mind reeling.

"I don't love easily or casually," he says as he finishes taking off my clothes. He holds me to him, naked and trembling.

He slings me up into his arms and walks to his room. I know where he's going before he takes me.

The closet.

Like the other room, the door to this one is hidden against the wall. If you didn't know it was there, you'd completely miss it.

His closet's actually locked. I stare as he slides his thumb to the panel and unlocks it before a second shot of laser scans his eyes. Holy shit. What does he have in here? I hold my breath, my body hot and supple against his fully clothed one.

It glides open. A dim yellow light illuminates the room. He shuts the door behind us with finality and I hear an audible *click*.

To call this place a closet would be like calling a lion a housecat.

Nicolette has told me about Fabien's bag of tricks, a closet he has outfitted with every disguise one could imagine, and not because Fabien likes to play dress-up.

Fabien has a fetish for heists, robbery, and trickery of all sorts.

Lyam has a fetish for pets... both the animal and human variety.

And Thayer? Holy hell.

It appears Thayer has a fetish for... *everything*.

SIXTEEN

Thayer

I've never brought a woman in here before.

There isn't a single goddamn thing in here any other woman's ever looked at, much less touched.

Savannah takes it all in with wide eyes. First, the corner of the room where I keep a lockbox with my weapons and the tools I use to clean them. A small stool where I sit to do the job.

Then the specialized toys I have on the walls—the whips and crops, paddles and handcuffs, gags and hoods. The specialized lingerie I've had designed just for her, in her favorite colors and textures and designs. The wooden spanking horse, decked out in Italian leather and fitted with padded straps.

"Holy shit, Thayer," she whispers, as I slide her down and let her explore. She reaches a tentative finger to a small pink feather. "What's this for?"

"Sensation play."

"And this?" she asks, pointing to a small shelf filled with enhancers and lubricants.

"Those are to heighten your experience."

She lifts a small bottle of elixir, reads the label, then returns it to the shelf.

Turning, she faces my arsenal. "And... this?"

"Those are my weapons."

"That you use," she says as if processing, as if trying to understand how I work and what I do. She's heard more about me than I ever planned on telling her at once, but I don't regret it. My only regret is that she didn't ask *me*.

"Of course."

Turning to face me, I wonder if she's forgotten she's naked. "So you use these?"

"Yes, when necessary."

"Well." She swallows and looks at the lockbox. "Can I open it?"

I nod. I've got tools and accessories to wipe prints and a full arsenal of ways to erase her identity if we ever needed to.

I'll do everything in my power to make sure we don't need to.

"The lock code is fourteen-ten."

She gives me a curious look. "October fourteenth?"

I nod. "The day my father died."

I don't ever want to forget what happened. It fuels me, to make me a better man.

I watch as her delicate fingers input the code and slide the lock open. The box is about the size of a small trunk, the boot of a car. Gingerly she removes one of the weapons, then another, eying them each in turn.

"I've never held a gun before," she whispers.

"How does it feel?"

I wonder if she'll drop it. Does she fear the use of a weapon?

Her voice is a low hum when she replies in a heated whisper, "I love it. It feels like it belongs here. I like the heft of it in my palm." Turning to me, her eyes grow heated as she begs me, "Teach me to use it, Thayer?"

I swear my dick gets harder just at the thought. "Teach you how to shoot? Of course. I promise you two things, love. First, you'll know how to shoot in no time because I'll personally teach you. Second, I'll make sure you never have to."

She places the weapon back into the box with care.

"Good girl," I approve. "Always treat a weapon as if it were loaded."

"Oh my God, I can't imagine how good this will be for my writing," she muses. "If I can describe —eeek!"

I come up behind her and lift her straight off the floor. I haven't forgotten why I brought her here, and I'm going to make damn sure she doesn't forget either.

"Now, let's explore the other side of the room. The side you know you're dying to get into."

"That scary wall with tools I know you're going to use on me? That wooden horse thing? The torture devices?"

I swallow hard while I crave her. "Yes. I want you to pick something out we'll use later. I have a job to do and some questions I need answering. I don't want you to witness what I have to do. I've got plenty of places for you to go to entertain yourself and stay out of trouble until I return."

"Are you sure about that?" she asks with a saucy toss of her head.

"Positive. Now go, before I change my mind."

"Gonna spank me, daddy?" she asks, sashaying toward the wall.

"You goddamn know it." *Fuck,* she makes me so damn hard.

I watch as she fingers a paddle, a length of silk-covered rope, a hood. She flicks a flogger against her palm and gets a wicked smile, then reaches for a pair of clamps.

"Wow," she whispers. "There's so much."

Crotchless panties and a silk negligee join the ensemble.

"Lay them across the horse and tell me what you want."

She takes her time walking to the horse, then lays them down neatly. Turning to me, her cheeks as flushed as her perfect little nipples, she whispers. "I want you to use me. I want you to tie me up and fuck me. I want you to show me, like you already have, where all this can take us."

"Perfect. Now come here."

When she reaches me, I lift her. I kiss her. I hold her pressed against me as I walk toward the wall and push her to it until her back is flush against it. I wrap her legs around me.

"You're so beautiful," I murmur in her ear. "Are you afraid, Savannah?"

"Yes," she whispers. "But it's not... the kind of fear that makes me want to run, Thayer. It's the kind that makes me want to hide, but I won't. I'm going to go on and face this head-on. If you think you're going to scare me away, you've got another thing coming."

"Is that right?" I feel my lips tip upward in a grin.

"That's right. You're not scaring me away."

I hate that I fight the need to push her away. If she walks down this path with me... if we take this road together... I don't know how I'll handle it if she has to walk away.

"I don't fuck for fun, Savannah. I want to make love to you. This is nothing casual. Do you understand me?"

I unzip my pants and remove my hard, throbbing cock. I shouldn't be here. I shouldn't be doing this right now. But I want her to know she's mine. I want her to know exactly who I am, and this time, if she doesn't turn away... if she doesn't run...

I want her to know exactly who *we* are together.

When I slide into her, she's so wet, I groan. Her pussy hugs my cock perfectly. Her legs anchor her to me as I kiss her and thrust, her body molded to mine. I love the way she arches her back and moans, the way she wants this as much as I do. I love the way she leans into me and takes me, just as I am, unencumbered by words or thoughts or fears, just the two of us bared and broken.

I love the way she feels when I come. I spill my seed in her as her own climax envelops her in nothing but pure, unadulterated ecstasy.

And I love the way her lips nestle against my neck, and she settles into me.

I want to tell her I love her. I want to know that she does, too.

With her arms wrapped around my shoulders and her damp cheek next to mine, my cock still in her while my seed spills from her and marks her naked skin, I make a promise.

"No matter what, Savannah. No matter who tries to come between us, no matter what they try to do, I promise you. I won't let them. No matter the cost." I grip her to me so hard she gasps. "Do you hear me? *No matter the cost.*"

"I hear you," she whispers, closing her eyes as she rests against me. "And I understand."

My cock pulses in her. The air smells like sex and danger and I want to fuck her all over again. I want her to feel me when she goes to bed at night and feel me when she wakes up in the morning.

I want her to know that I love her.

"Get dressed," I tell her in her ear. "Don't clean up. I want you to know when you go out there who you belong to. I want you to remember the way I fucked you." I turn her to look at the spanking horse with the toys lined up. "I want you to remember exactly what we need to do when we get back here tonight. Do you understand me?"

"I do," she whispers. "Yes, sir."

I kiss her and hold her.

I wish I could hold her here forever.

SEVENTEEN

Savannah

The next two weeks with Thayer are the most thrilling, exciting days of my life. I never knew it could be like this.

It feels like I've taken a two-week vacation, only I don't have any hope of returning to normalcy.

Thayer has shown me the deeper, darker side of things I never knew existed, and now that I know, I will never go back to anything shallow and superficial.

And most definitely anything vanilla.

That first night, he had me wait for him. And when he returned, he looked like a man coming back from war. I didn't want to ask what he had done. I didn't want to know.

I remember what he's said, what he's done. I can't let myself forget it.

He's taken me out privately to teach me to shoot and says I'm a natural. I love the heft of a pistol in my hands, the feel of his body behind me, the thrill that races through me when I hit my target.

But as the days pass, I realize that we're not getting anywhere.

They haven't discovered the security breach. And it appears that the people after me actually believe the decoy was me. Nicolette plays her part of the mourning sister, and the Gerards pretend they're looking for who did it but failing.

All seems quiet, but I don't know if we can trust it.

How long is this situation going to keep me under lock and key? What if the days string into weeks and the weeks into months?

I talk to my sister and Cosette and Gwen, my sister's friend and another employee here.

It's a small circle of friends but I love them.

I love my new hairstyle, and I am really in love with this club. It isn't just the luxurious accommodations, or the feeling like I wake up every day in a bed-and-breakfast. It's so much more.

It's the deep, intimate, relationships I witness firsthand on a daily basis. It's the knowledge that

Thayer, as master and owner of this club, won't let so much as a stray mouse inside these premises without permission. And I know deep down inside, above all, it's the feeling of safety.

But I can't help but wonder if it's a false sense of security. Am I only safe if I'm hidden? How long will he hide me?

At first, I wondered with every day that passed if I would feel more secure in our relationship. But it seems to be having the opposite effect.

He won't take me into a public room. All our meals are ordered and sent to his private suite.

And even though this is a spacious place to be, I miss Paris. I miss who I was in Paris, I miss being a grad student. I miss strolling alongside the Seine. I even miss shopping. Anything I need, he sends here, but it isn't the same.

And even though being with Thayer is the sexiest thing I've ever done, a part of me wants to see what else this club has to offer.

I want more.

I don't like not knowing where the danger lies, and I don't just mean the people who are after me. Sometimes I feel as if Thayer paws the ground, like a bull ready to charge.

I don't know if I want to be the one waving the red flag when he does.

One day, a couple weeks after we arrived, Thayer leaves me for a few hours. When he returns, he doesn't tell me where he was or what he did. I don't usually ask questions, but this time I do. I want to know how long this interminable wait will continue.

"So. Do you have any more leads? Any more talk about where I am or who I am?"

"No."

"Do they still think the decoy was me?"

"I'm not sure."

I blow out a breath. "How will you be sure? How much longer will this be?"

"Will what be?"

I gesture around the room. "Staying hidden like this. I feel some days like the walls are closing in on me."

He gives me a long look.

"As long as it takes."

I sigh impatiently and clench my jaw. I'm not surprised when he walks over to me and makes me look at him by taking my chin in his hand. "What's going on?"

"I don't want to hide anymore, Thayer. I miss going outside. I miss being able to do things like shop, and go to class, and grab some pastry at a bakery. I miss socializing and parties and all the things I used to do."

I don't know how to tell him that I fear I'm not enough for him. Will I ever be enough, or am I just a passing fling to him? I still can't help but wonder if he needs someone like one of those stunningly beautiful submissives, or one of the willing servants.

A part of me wonders what he does when he's not with me.

"Savannah."

"I don't like being here, all alone," I tell him. "I don't..." I look away from him then, because I suddenly don't feel good. I feel like I'm going to cry, and I hate that. I don't like feeling like my emotions are getting the best of me. I shake my head. "I don't wanna talk right now."

I wonder if he's going to make me talk because he doesn't allow me to hold anything back from him. I believe that good communication skills are essential in any working relationship, but I wonder if sometimes he needs to respect my privacy.

"Are you okay?"

I look away.

"I have a little bit of a headache. Probably just getting my period."

Frowning, he takes his phone out of his pocket. "I'm calling a doctor."

And that's Thayer. He is the most overprotective human I've ever met in my life. An utter perfectionist, he dots every *i* and crosses every *t* and leaves no room whatsoever for error.

He's not calling the doctor for a *headache*.

"I don't need to see a doctor. It's just a headache. I get them sometimes."

He gives me a sharp look. "And you're just telling me this now?"

I shrug. "Why would I randomly tell you I sometimes get headaches when I've been reading too much or staring at my computer screen all day long?"

But then he gives me one of those looks, one I know all too well tells me he is not arguing the point. I roll my eyes and cave. "Fine. Call the doctor, who is probably just going to give me some pain meds and tell me to make sure I'm hydrated." I turn away from him because if he sees me rolling my eyes again, I'm going to land over his knee. And I'm not feeling it.

"Are you well hydrated?"

I speak through gritted teeth. *"Yes."*

A few minutes later, the doctor arrives. She's a slight woman in her late fifties or so, with a smattering of gray in her head of curls. We go through every routine question from my sexual history to when was the last time I got my period.

When *did* I last get my period. I have an odd sense of time since coming here.

"It's a *headache*." Dear God, overreact much?

Thayer hovers in the background, and I can't help but think. If I'm pregnant... My God, if I'm pregnant, he's going to lock me up in a cave somewhere and throw away the key.

Would it be too early to tell?

Suddenly, I don't want him to know and I'm not sure why. I need to find out this news alone.

"Thayer, can you give us some privacy?" I ask, knowing full well he won't.

"Privacy?" He looks at me as if I just asked if he would please take a little trip to the moon.

"I want to talk to her about girl things," I explain, and it isn't a lie.

"Girl things," he repeats, staring me down.

"It's a patient's prerogative, Mr. Gerard," the doctor says gently. I mentally fist-bump her.

Thayer scowls at both of us. If he really wanted to, he could refuse.

He doesn't though. "Fine. I'll be back in ten minutes."

The door closes behind him with a resounding thud.

As soon as we're alone, I turn to face her.

"How did you come to work here?" I want to know who she really is.

Is she a slave? Or a master?

She faces me calmly. Not the first time she's gotten this question, I'm guessing. "I am a kink-friendly physician. I don't participate in anything at this club, but I don't judge any of the things that go on either. The Gerard family is very important to me. They saved me from a very dark place, and I am in their debt. They pay me well, and I make sure that I tend to any wounds or illnesses that come this way." She gives me a knowing smile. "Whether they be dungeon-related or otherwise."

Excellent. So she does things like bandage the lacerations on his knuckles when he gives someone a beatdown? Removes bullets embedded in his flesh? Isn't that lovely.

I remember what Nicolette told me. I remember what Thayer told me.

Thayer is unlike anyone I've ever met before, and never pretends to be someone he's not. He's raw, primal, and *all mine*. He's brutal and savage, fierce in a way that satisfies a need deep within me. He's everything I fear and everything I crave. He scares me yet makes me feel safer than I ever knew possible. He makes me question what I know. Who I am. But more than anything… he's becoming one of my best friends.

There's a raw honesty about him that makes me realize there's nothing I can't tell him. And when he strips me of all that troubles me, he makes me vulnerable and unprotected, but doesn't leave me there.

God, I love this man. I really think I do.

But the question is… does he love me back?

"Can I ask you a question?"

She nods placidly. "Of course you can."

"What if I'm… pregnant?"

The doctor smiles. "We were getting there. I'd offer you congratulations."

"No, but… well… would you have to tell Thayer? Isn't there something about patient confidentiality or something?"

"Of course," she says with concern. "Though he is the one that employs me, and I typically advise patients under my care to inform their partner." She pauses. "Am I guessing this would be an unwanted pregnancy?"

"No. I mean, yes. Oh, God, I don't know." I feel cold and hot, and am I imagining things or am I actually nauseous, too?

She gives me another smile. "You'd be surprised how often I hear that."

Oh no I wouldn't.

"And this is one of the reasons why I would advise you that it's probably best to tell Mr. Gerard either way. If you were, say, pregnant and hid it from him, you wouldn't want to engage in a scene that could harm you."

"Such as...?"

I'm definitely nauseous.

"There aren't many scenarios, but breath play is one of them. It's very important. You'd want to proceed with caution with impact play as well, and I definitely wouldn't advise anything that would involve your nipples, not that it would cause any harm to a baby, but because you might fly right out of your skin."

"Got it."

Baby.

Baby?

"Lots of women have babies when they're into this lifestyle," she says.

Uh, okay.

I need to know what's going on, and I need to know *now*.

"If I'm pregnant, I need to swear you to secrecy. For now, anyway."

She nods, though she looks a bit apprehensive about this concept. "Of course."

I can't tell her why, but a part of me fears that if I find out I'm pregnant, he'll stay with me out of loyalty. That's who he is, fiercely protective and loyal to a fault.

I want to be cherished, not kept out of obligation.

I want to love and be loved, not paired with someone who could never truly love me back.

I'm too young for him, too naïve, and he deserves someone who could truly meet his needs.

If I'm pregnant and I stay with him, I'll never know... was it loyalty or love that kept us together? I don't want him to stay with me out of a sheer sense of loyalty. *I want to know that he chose me.*

After all I've been through–the loss of my parents and having to go it alone, learning how to adult without the presence of anyone to emulate or learn from, distance from Nicolette, even though I'll never fault her for trying to provide for me—I can't risk being left all over again.

I can't spend the rest of my life wondering if he truly loves me.

Especially not by the only man I've ever loved.

I need distance and clarity and time, no matter what that test reveals.

I realize I'm pacing the room, tugging on the collar Thayer put on me the night in the glass-paneled room and has yet to remove. I finger the metal and give it a tug. He likes to play with it and caress it when we make love. There was a time when the sturdiness of it gave me comfort, a physical reminder of his presence and love. But now...

As she's packing up her things, the doctor frowns and points to the metal collar.

"I don't want to overstep," she says quietly, with a note of concern that paints her voice. "But are you aware that this is a tracking device?"

I stop pacing. "A what?"

"Tracking device," she repeats. I know what the words mean but somehow have a hard time making it all click. "Exactly the same as they use on pets to track their whereabouts in the event of an escape." She frowns. "Normally I'd keep my opinions to myself, but if you're pregnant... it could prove risky." She bites her lip before she continues. It occurs to me then, and I'm not sure why it took me so long to realize this—she's afraid of Thayer.

"What else?" I whisper, while my mind still plays with the concept of him *tracking me like I'm an animal.*

"It doesn't come off easily, for one. It has to be removed with wire cutters and could inhibit circulation in the event of an emergency. Another—"

"Take it off," I interrupt. I don't want to hear another word. I don't need to hear about the risks. I want it *off*.

How could he? After all we've been through, after all I've surrendered to him. I've trusted him implicitly and he doesn't trust me at all?

She sighs and nods. "Of course. I can do that. I'll have to fetch an instrument we use in an emergency situation to remove rings on swollen fingers or the like. I know we keep one in some of the playroom emergency kits." She looks around her as if expecting Thayer to come storming in here, before she shakes her head. "I'll be back soon."

I sit, staring into nothingness. I feel numb as I wait for her, the new knowledge of his actions and the impending results of the test I'm going to take weighing me down, muddling my thoughts, stirring up feelings that I don't like.

She isn't gone long, likely moving as fast as she can so she can be done with this and hightail it out of here before he returns.

I glance at the time. He'll be back any second now.

I close my eyes, my cheeks damp with tears, when she cuts the clasp.

I hate the feeling of the collar coming off. I don't like the way it looks in her hands, broken and clipped, as if it symbolizes our severed union. A bird with broken wings, unable to fly.

Before I go—and I have to go—I need to know one thing.

I know what I have to do.

I tell myself I'm free now. No longer encumbered with anything that will weigh me down.

But I don't feel free. I don't at all. I feel... alone.

I square my shoulders and face the doctor. "Alright, then. Let's take that test."

EIGHTEEN

Thayer

I check the time and watch the seconds tick by. I said ten minutes. Time's up.

I'm walking toward my room to see if she's okay when I hear my name.

"Thayer!" I turn to find Cosette in the lobby flagging me down. "Lyam says he needs you in the break room."

Her widened eyes tell me something's wrong.

"Is everything okay?"

Her brows draw together, and she shakes her head. "I don't know."

Dammit. I send Savannah a text.

Me:

> I went to check on you, but Lyam called. I'll be there in a few minutes.

She doesn't respond.

I walk quickly to the break room, located behind the lobby. Lyam's with our head of security and a few of our other guards. They have a tablet in front of them.

Lyam's uncharacteristically grim. "Thayer, there's been another security breach. You know we never discovered who it was last time and chalked it up to being a glitch in the system." He scowls. "But it's clear someone's bypassed our security measures."

"So someone's in the club unannounced?" I ask, making a quick mental tally of the weapons I have on hand.

Lyam's gaze darkens. He's as ruthless as I am, only Lyam has much more creative methods than I do.

I shake my head. "Lock down all community rooms."

"Already done."

"I want a list of every guest we have on the premises as well as their partners, and every staff member who's checked in today. If they're here to cut the grass or dust the goddamn chandeliers, I want their names."

"On it."

Lyam flicks his finger across a tablet, and it springs to life. He taps and scrolls, pinches and pulls. Seconds later, my phone dings with a text.

"That was fast."

"I was already on it before you arrived."

Savannah.

"I need to check on Savannah." I jerk my chin to our head of security and his chief operator. "You sweep the first quadrant, Lyam and I will sweep the second through fourth."

"Yessir."

They quickly rise, weapons drawn. This is no conventional club where I make everyone keep weapons secured. If we need them, we use them, which is partly why we rarely need to.

"Do we have any leads at all? Anything out of place?"

Lyam shakes his head. "That's the bitch of it, nothing at all."

Fuck it. I'm getting Savannah before we do any sweep at all.

There's a tentative knock at the door. I stand and flick on the overhead security camera. Cosette stands there, wringing her hands. "Sir?"

"Yes?" Lyam and I both say in unison. I give him a sharp look then blow out a breath. He's not allowed to consort with our employees, so I wonder what's going on, but we have no time to talk about it.

"May I come in?"

I open the door to let her in, even while I'm ready to burst out of here and check on Savannah. I don't like feeling like I'm being held back from locating her. Cosette comes in, her cheeks flushed and eyes bright. "I'm so sorry to interrupt," she says. Something's off. I can't put my finger on it, but something isn't quite right.

"What is it?" I want to shake her to get her to say what's on her mind so I can get out of here.

"The girls' dressing room," she says. "There were various outfits out of place, sir." She looks as if she's going to be sick.

My phone buzzes with a text and I want to whip it against the wall.

"Look into that," I snap at Lyam as the two of them head out.

I won't investigate another damn thing until I have her safely beside me. The fear I had from the very beginning rears its ugly head. I don't want to leave anything to chance. I don't want to lose the woman I love.

I make it back to our room and yank open the door. "Savannah!"

No answer. My heart threatens to pound out of my chest as I quickly scan the room. No sign of a struggle or an intrusion, but she's nowhere to be seen.

"*Savannah!*"

I call her phone and it goes to voicemail. I'm pacing, racking my brain to see if I can remember which camera will show me where she went, when I see a folded piece of paper on the small entryway table next to my keys. When I pick it up, I see the broken, mangled collar.

No.

A cold feeling of dread washes through me. I pick it up and unfold it.

> *Thayer,*
>
> *I found out about the collar. You can keep it.*
>
> *I want to thank you for everything you've done for me. But I can't stay*

here hiding any longer. If you had your way, I'd be under lock and key for the rest of my life, and I can't do that anymore. I'm not an animal to be locked up and tracked. I'm a human being with a will of her own. It's probably fruitless to ask, but I'm going to anyway.

Please don't look for me.

Savannah

I wad up the paper and whip it against the wall.

Where did she go?

What the fuck is she thinking?

Earlier today, she started pushing back against my insistence that she stay safe and secure. I know she's sick of being here and wants more, but she hasn't seen what I have. She doesn't know how vindictive our enemies are. I can't let her go until I know they're no longer a threat.

I pick up my phone to have Lyam scan footage when a text comes through.

Nicolette:

> I picked Savannah up and I'm taking her to the spa for the day. I promise she's in good hands

Me:

> Not yet, I want to see her first

There's no reply. What the fuck is going on here?

The spa. They're at the spa? She hasn't left, then?

I walk through the hotel lobby, and everything seems normal, nothing out of place. Heading into the weekend, we have more guests than we do on weekdays, so it's busy, but we have staff that handles everything from bags to check-in to guest room services.

The spa. I have to get to the spa, if that's where she's gone.

I blow out a breath, trying to calm my nerves. I'm not normally a nervous person, but this time... Why does it feel like I'm on a wild goose chase?

I call her, but it goes to her voicemail.

I'm practically running by the time I get to the spa and haven't even checked my quadrant yet. My phone buzzes with texts from our security men and Lyam. Nothing out of place.

Where is she?

The very thing I feared feels as if it's looming, a wild animal with bared fangs, ready to pounce.

I've been in this position before with people I love being threatened or in danger. I can still see the flames leaping from the building, the roof collapsing. I can still imagine my father's screams before he died.

I can still feel the way I held his broken body when I finally got to him.

I need to find her. I need to keep her safe. I'll do whatever it takes.

I call Fabien, who answers on the first ring.

"Why the fuck is your wife taking Savannah out without my permission, and why the fuck isn't she answering her phone? And was she the one that told her about that fucking collar?"

There's a brief pause. "Excuse me?"

"Fabien." I blow out a breath. "Nicolette texted me that she was taking Savannah to the spa. I didn't give Savannah permission to leave the room, and we've got a suspected security breach here. I left her for ten goddamn minutes. No fucking way am I okay with Nicolette sauntering in here and just—"

"Thayer." Fabien's voice cuts through my ranting. I pause.

"What?"

"Nicolette's phone broke last night. She dropped it in the bath, and we ordered another one. She's here, right next to me. We're in Paris."

My vision swims in sudden rage.

"What?"

"Thayer?" Nicolette's panicked voice screams on the other end of the phone. "Is my sister okay? Thayer, tell me Savannah's okay!"

I hang up the phone and run to the spa. I know what I'll find before I get there.

I reach the spa, yank open the door, and nearly scare the shit out of clients in robes drinking tea in the waiting room. I march to the desk. The hostess stares at me, her mouth open.

"Sir? Is everything okay?"

I already know the answer before I ask the question.

"Show me your guest list."

"We only have four guests at the moment, sir, and they're in our waiting room."

Someone set me up. Someone's breached our security and entered the club and set me up.

Savannah's gone.

The sudden wailing of sirens makes everyone sit up straighter. I clench my jaw.

I need to find Savannah.

I need to find the security breach.

I need to find out why the fuck we have police here.

Fucking hell.

I leave the spa and head to the lobby as an entire rash of armed police officers swarms the lobby. Guests stand, frozen in place. We've never had officers in here before, and we keep our location secured.

"Thayer Gerard?"

I nod, guarded and on edge.

No. They can't be here for me. Not here, not now, not when I need to secure Savannah.

Six officers come at me at once, like I'm a goddamned threat. "You're under arrest for the murder of Officer Charlemont Laguerre." My head swims with questions.

They're framing me for the murder? Of fucking *course* they are. Frame me. Have me taken away, where I can't come after them and murder them with my bare hands for even looking at my woman.

I quickly run through my options of escape but know immediately that if I fight them now, I'll never find Savannah. With every fiber of my being screaming against me, I grit my teeth when they cuff me.

Lyam enters the lobby. He stares, unblinking.

I yell over my shoulder as they take me out, "I'm innocent. Take over in my stead. Fucking find Savannah and call our lawyer, in that order."

NINETEEN

Savannah

I can't believe he fucking *tracked me*.

Okay, I can, if I think about it. It's not really out of character at all, but I can't believe I let myself fall for anything that even resembled love, because I know now, he doesn't love me. He doesn't trust me. He kept me as his little pet, someone he could manipulate and control, but no more.

Not with these stakes.

I'm not the kind of person to sneak around. I hate leaving him a note, but I know Thayer. If I tell him to his face that I need space and time to think things over, he's not going to let me leave. He won't let me go out on my own, no matter what security measures I take, because he doesn't believe that I'd be safe. He'd wrap me in bubble wrap if he could.

And I have a lot to think about. Oh, God, so much to think about. It isn't just *me* anymore.

I pinch the bridge of my nose, trying to quell the rising tide of emotion that threatens to strangle me. I draw in a breath and let it out slowly and think about my options.

I have no idea where I am, so leaving scares me. He blindfolded me when we came here, so I don't know our exact location, but I do know we're in Corsica.

I call Nicolette, but the call goes to voicemail. I consider calling Fabien, but I don't know if he's more loyal to his brother or his wife, so I don't trust that option, either.

After the doctor left, I had some decisions to make. I pause before leaving the closet, thinking about what my next steps should be. Ignoring all the little trinkets and mementos of our play, and the way the whole closet smells like Thayer, I wonder what would be the easiest way for me to leave. Then I remember what Nicolette told me. Fabien has a large stash of secret identities, for him and for her. If I could get my hands on one of the fake ID's, I could take a flight.

My mind races with possibilities and plans.

I'll have to get away from here, whether I walk or somehow con my way into getting a ride. From there, I have to get to Paris.

The garden.

I could get to the garden from here and access GPS with a burner phone, call a ride, and head to one of the hotels in Corsica. I know which ones the Gerards own and which ones they don't. Even if there was someone watching my every move, as he seems to think there is, I can sneak out that way.

No. I need to get to Paris, where I have more options. It's not hard to get to Paris from Corsica. The biggest obstacle is actually leaving Le Luxe.

I hate sneaking, and would much rather just face this head-on, but I know how he is and what he'll do.

I feel like I'm going to be sick, and this time I can't blame the hormones. After everything we've been through, everything we've shared—and now the news I got today that will change everything—it feels as if I'm leaving a part of my own heart behind.

I know that I can't trust feelings, that I need to rely on the next best logical move.

Gain clarity.

Step away.

Stay safe.

It's time.

Just as a precaution, I wear one of my wigs and decide to take one of the weapons from the closet. I slide the slim pistol he's taught me to use in the side of a boot, in a little holster he's had fashioned for that exact purpose. I've never been allowed to use it without him, but I'm ready. I find a stash of cash he's got tucked into a bedside drawer and slide it into my bra.

For the love of God, I can't believe he *tracked* me.

No more. *No more.*

I walk with purpose and confidence, so no one stops me on the way to the library, not a soul coming between me and my mission to escape.

Escape, like I'm a caged animal. I stifle the sudden need to cry.

I look around me with a growing sense of loss. I don't want to leave the comfort and security of Le Luxe. I don't want to leave Thayer.

I like it here.

To think... I thought I loved him.

On the way to the library, I casually walk by the bank of offices on the first floor, near one of the playrooms. I know Nicolette told me her change of clothes, and the disguises and false identities, were close.

Bingo. Feeling like a kid escaping from a store with a candy bar, I find one that looks closest to my disguise and slide the false passport into my pocket.

When I reach the library, I close the door behind me.

Sirens wail outside.

Sirens?

From the doorway I can see police vehicles surrounding the entrance to Le Luxe.

Oh, God. Have I made a mistake coming here?

Why is my first thought of Thayer?

I remind myself that I don't need him to protect me. I can take care of myself.

At the sight of the police officers exiting their vehicles, my mind goes back to that night. I can still see the man they killed, crumpled and sprawled on the ground as blood seeped out of him onto the pavement, taking his life with it.

This isn't a casual visit but a raid.

"Savannah?"

I look over my shoulder to see Cosette enter the library.

Shit.

I paste a smile on my face. Ugh. I have to get rid of her. "Hey. What's going on?"

"I'm sorry," she says, her face drawn as she shakes her head. "I'm really sorry."

I give her a curious look. Why is she apologizing?

Movement outside catches my attention. Moments later, my heart leaps into my throat when I see Thayer being taken out in handcuffs. He has a look of stoic but grim determination on his face. Lyam prowls behind him, his phone to his ear.

Seeing him like this—helpless, under arrest—confirms my worst fear. He isn't a man I can trust. Thayer can't keep me safe anymore. This time, I allow myself the momentary weakness of shedding a tear. I wipe my cheeks and turn to face Cosette.

I stare for a moment, unsure of what I'm seeing. Cosette behind me, trembling, a syringe poised in her hand, ready to strike.

Adrenaline surges through me. I knock the syringe from her hand on instinct. She screams and sobs.

"They'll kill him, Savannah, kill them all!" she chokes. "You have to let me!"

"Let you kill me? Oh hell no. What the *fuck*, Cosette? This isn't you!"

"It's—it won't kill you, I promise." Yeah, she's not talking me into that. When I shake my head at her, she lunges for me and I duck just in time, sending her sprawling onto one of the sofas. It's been a while since I've taken self-defense, but I remember the basics. I don't want to hurt her, but I can deflect.

Cosette isn't a fighter, and she doesn't want to hurt me either, but whoever "they" are have convinced her she has to. With my heart threatening to pound out of my chest, I launch myself at her.

"Please," she begs as she falls to the floor. I feel sick. I don't notice the syringe is back in her hand until she tries to stab me with it. *No.*

I have to get out of here.

I lift my arm and deflect her. When she stumbles, I elbow her, trying to ignore her cry of pain. I hate this, but I have to get out of here. I wrestle the syringe out of her hand, hold her, and feel tears blur my vision.

She said it won't kill me. It's for sedation then.

"I'm sorry," I whisper, before I sink the needle into her neck, shove her away, and run. She falls to the floor with a cry.

I yank the handle that leads to the garden, but it's locked. I'm desperate to get out as Cosette stumbles behind me, coming after me. She sinks to her knees, her head wobbling from side to side.

"They're going to kill me," she whispers. "They're going to kill us all. I'm sorry. I'll cover for you as long as I can." She sobs openly, falling forward on her hands.

I remember the passcode to Thayer's lockbox and enter it as quickly as I can. I stifle a sob when the door opens. The date of his father's death leads me out of here.

The garden's vacant, but not far from here I can see the police cars. The flashing lights. Uniformed officers talking in clipped tones. I hide in a crouched position until they're gone, scanning my surroundings.

I've hardly been out here. I don't know where I am.

I call Nicolette on the burner phone again, but it still goes to voicemail. My stomach clenches in fear. Where is she?

In the distance, I see a sleek black car pull up to the curb and an elegant couple dressed in formal attire steps out. My heart races. They have a driver.

I wait until they enter Le Luxe before I jog to the car. The driver stares at me in shock when I point my gun at him.

"Get out of the car," I say in a rush of words, "and I won't hurt you."

Ugh, I feel absolutely terrible threatening anyone at all. It feels so unnatural. "And I promise you'll be compensated," I add as an afterthought. I think of Cosette, Thayer being taken, Nicolette, and my need to stay safe, and a rush of adrenaline surges me forward. "Now!"

He leaves in a rush as voices shout behind me. I slide into the driver's seat, my hands quaking as I think about what I have to do next, drive into the unknown. Fend for myself. Leave everything behind.

Does this complicate things with my sister? How could it not?

But first, I have to get away.

The first thing I notice is that Le Luxe is set behind rows and rows of tall pines, their evergreen needles forming a veritable wall behind which the club hides. The second is that I've never seen this place before in my life.

My heart's in my throat when I gun the engine, the need for speed propelling me forward. Thankfully, the luxury car handles like a dream, as I take turns with quick jerks of the wheel. The yells of the people behind me fade as I pick up speed until I get to a main road.

Silence. Nothing but the hum of the engine and an open road before me.

I'm too wound up and anxious to cry, but I give myself permission to release a shuddering breath.

It doesn't help.

I look around me and realize I'm alone. Completely and utterly alone. The road in front of me blurs. I swipe at tears and will myself to stay calm, to stay focused, and to get the hell out of here.

Hours later, I pull into the outskirts of the airport parking lot with a plan. The entire time, I waited for someone to chase me down, for sirens or even a helicopter to come after me like I'm their most wanted criminal. But no one came. I'm not exactly a getaway driver, so I assume either the couple whose car I stole doesn't want to pursue me, or someone stopped them.

My heart aches and my stomach rumbles.

I call Nicolette again but get no answer.

It's about seventeen hours to drive from here to Paris, and it involves a ferry. The longer it takes me to get there the more of a chance I'd be caught. At this point, I'm not even sure how many people are after me.

I need to get to Paris alone, without help.

Flying is the quickest option, but if anyone's after me and boards a plane with me, I have no means of escape. I also can't take any weapons on a plane.

So I decide to drive. I feel like a fugitive as I rely on caffeine to propel me forward.

I can do this.

I have to.

I abandon the car before I board the ferry and thankfully make it aboard with no one following me. I scroll through the phone to try to see why Thayer's been arrested, but I see nothing.

I send Nicolette another text.

No response.

Hours later, I'm almost to what I'd call home.

I close my eyes, pretending to sleep on the ferry, and try to formulate a plan, but my thoughts keep going back to Thayer and Nicolette.

My family.

I hoped landing in Paris would give me some measure of reassurance, but I'm sorely disappointed. I still feel bereft.

I should be here with Thayer.

Thayer.

Why did they take him? I hate that I've left him in Corsica, but I've almost made him up in my mind to be a sort of superhero, who can handle anyone or anything that comes his way.

Thayer can take care of Thayer.

Still, I hate that I'm running. I want things back to where they were, where they should be.

I check my messages when we pull into dock, and my heart swells when I see a reply from my sister.

NICOLETTE:

> Savannah! Where are you?

I can't hide things from my sister, but I don't trust her not to tell her husband.

Me:

> I had to leave. What is happening? Is Cosette okay? Thayer?

Nicolette:

> OMG, girl. Thayer's been arrested for the murder of the officer!!!!

My heart thumps wildly in my chest. She hasn't answered about Cosette.

They had him framed for the murder of the officer.

No.

"Hey. Excuse me, are you going to move or what?" A grumpy middle-aged man with a bushy moustache scowls at me. I move out of his way and go to a vacated part of the lot. I scan my surroundings, looking all over the place for some kind of a threat, but I'm not Thayer or his brothers. I have no idea what I'd even be looking for.

I duck into a bathroom stall, seeking momentary safety.

Nicolette:

> Where are you?

Me:

> I can't tell you. I'm safe.

Nicolette:

> You have to tell me where you are. Now.

My stomach flips uneasily.

Something doesn't feel right. Nicolette didn't answer my question about Cosette, and she doesn't text like this. Has Fabien taken over her phone?

I decide to test it.

Me:

> I told you I'm safe. I need some time alone. Just make sure that someone takes care of Blubbers, okay?

Nicolette:

> Of course. Now tell me where you are.

Anger flashes through me. I narrow my eyes at the phone.

My fish's name is Van Gogh. Who the hell is this?

Did they take my sister? Have they hurt her?

I send a quick text.

Me:

> Call me

No response.

I exit and look around me. It appears I'm alone, that no one's followed me.

Have I made a mistake leaving Corsica?

The Gerard family home is in walking distance of the ferry.

I wish it was the sanctuary to me it once was.

I walk down a shaded part of the Seine, trying to sort this all out and breathe deeply.

Freaking out right now solves nothing, so I have to stay in control. I can freak out later when I'm alone.

Does Fabien know Nicolette's been compromised?

TWENTY

Savannah

I HAVE TO FIND NICOLETTE.

And Thayer...

If someone's taken Nicolette and someone's framed Thayer... my flat in Paris isn't safe anymore. I'll never forgive myself if my sister's hurt. *It's my fault.*

I take a left down a side street and look at the rows upon rows of vendors, one of my favorite places in Paris. I don't feel at home this time.

For the first time in my life, I feel homeless. Alone.

I tell myself that I'll get through this. But I don't have the option of giving up anymore. I need to do everything I can for the people I... love.

Do I love Thayer?

It's hard to imagine spending the rest of my life with a man so ruthless and hard.

But he softens when he's with me.

It's hard to imagine being with a man who doesn't trust me, who feels like I'm an object worthy of hoarding and hiding so he can have me all to himself.

Is that really why he tracked me?

I know, even as I'm doing it, that I'm trying to talk myself out of loving him. I'm trying to logic my way out of what I know in my heart is right.

I remember that night in the room made of glass.

I remember the first time I saw through that stern exterior and realized how much he loved me.

I remember the safety of his arms, the certainty of his loyalty, the warmth of his love.

And as I walk down the streets so familiar to me I've practically worn grooves in the pavement, I face my biggest fear of all: *If I go all in with Thayer, will he, too, leave me?*

I can't think about this now. I have to defend him in the name of what's right and just.

Maybe we aren't meant to be together. The thought makes my heart ache in a way I never knew possible.

I want to see him again. I want to look in his eyes and sit on his lap and frame his face in my hands so I can hold his gaze on me forever.

I want to remember what we had. I don't want to forget. For the first time in my life I felt loved and accepted just as I was. For the first time in my life, I felt cherished.

I shake myself out of my self-pity and face what's next.

I have to find my sister.

I push myself on and give myself the pep talk no one else is here to give me.

One day this will all be behind you.

This will all be put to rights, and soon.

Sometimes, a girl just needs to remember that the darkest places aren't here to stay. It's the reminder I need even as I feel my heart being rent in two.

I turn down another side street and am trying to quell the rapid beating of my pulse so I can solidify a plan when I notice a polished silver Porsche driving toward me.

I know it's no accident.

Are they following me? I frantically look for a place to hide when I hear the car accelerate.

There's no easy escape.

I can't let them take me. If they take me, they win. Thayer goes to jail and Nicolette's at their mercy.

I have to run.

I take a second to grab my gun and cock it as car doors open and I'm swarmed by armed men.

No.

I swivel to face them, my gun hand shaking.

"Leave me alone!" I yell in French. "Back off or I shoot!"

They stand still and one holds up a cell phone. "We've got her in front of us and she's armed."

A voice comes over the speakerphone. "Savannah, it's Lyam, get in the car and I'll explain everything."

My heart pounds.

Lyam?

My voice wavers. "How do I know you're not compromised?"

Lyam curses. "You have to trust me. Now get in the fucking car before someone catches you with that weapon and arrests you, too."

They know where I am and have somehow tracked me, so I can't escape. I can't go to my flat, and I definitely can't run.

Maybe sometimes the only choice is to take a leap of faith. To trust. Maybe sometimes it means defying all logic and leaping into the unknown with nothing but your parachute strapped to your back. Leaping into the air and pulling the cord, believing that you'll land on two feet.

I'll settle for not dying.

I point my gun down and remember where my knife is.

Lyam wouldn't betray his family. I may not know him as well as Thayer or Fabien, but I know that Lyam would rather die than betray the people he loves.

I can trust him.

"I'll go but I keep my weapons."

"You keep your weapons pointed away from my men."

Jesus, they're all the same.

"Fine."

I get in the car. Two men flank me, their weapons drawn, as the rest climb into the car. One taps his phone and seconds later, Mario and Lyam are on a screen.

My heartbeat slows and I blow out a tight breath. I recognize Le Luxe in the background.

Thank God I made the right decision.

I need to tell him what I know, and I need to resist any attempt he might make at bringing me back to Thayer.

I speak in a sudden rush of words, frantic to catch him up to speed and get help with what I have to do.

"Lyam! I think Nicolette's been taken."

He shakes his head. "She hasn't. I just spoke with her. She's with Fabien."

I close my eyes as a rush of emotion chokes me. I want to cry with relief.

Nicolette's okay. I open my eyes and draw in a deep breath. "Someone texted me from her number."

He sits up straighter. "Did they?" He and Mario share a look I don't quite understand.

"How can that happen?"

"It's not hard," Lyam says, reminding me that he's all-too-familiar with underhanded techie tactics. "It can be done on a computer by using the person's cell phone number. In our case, we're lucky Nicolette broke her phone, because now we know immediately the text wasn't from her."

Ahh.

"So someone wanted to find out where I was." I frown. "How did *you* know where I was?"

Lyam scowls into the screen, looking not unlike his brothers. "Do you think my brother was stupid enough to use only a collar as a tracking device on you?"

I stare at my body, as if an arrow with the word *tracker* would flash.

"How did you know about that?"

Lyam blows out an impatient breath. Now he definitely looks like Thayer. "Savannah, the trackers he put on you were in case of abduction, not because he thought he couldn't trust you." He shakes his head. "Jesus. The phone you're carrying has a tracker. The knife and gun have trackers. Even the clothing and wig have tracking devices embedded in them."

I feel my eyes go wide at this.

"And that haircut Cosette gave you? She wasn't just cutting your hair."

I stare at him before I trace my fingers around my scalp, looking for a microchip or something that would give it away.

"You won't find it. Thayer spent a lot of money making sure you wouldn't."

I slam my lips together and stare at the handle of the car door, wondering how I can escape from his hired help, but Lyam sees me.

"I watched footage of you leaving. If I hadn't been so distracted by Thayer's arrest, I would've prevented that. Why did you leave?"

"I don't owe you answers," I begin, but he shakes his head.

"Don't you see what's going on here? They framed Thayer as the murderer to draw you out. The Chabert family knows that you're a couple, and taking Thayer into custody was the best way they had to convince you to come forward. They couldn't storm the castle and take you, not from a place as secure as Le Luxe."

"And yet Cosette tried, didn't she?"

"Cosette?" Lyam asks. "What do you mean?"

I tell him everything that happened. He curses and lifts his phone, sends a few messages, then returns back to me with effort. He keeps glancing at his phone.

Are Lyam and Cosette a thing?

"First things first," he says. "Thayer put these trackers on you so I could find you if he was hurt, because that's the only damn way he'd let you go. I know you're in Paris, and as luck would have it, so are Fabien and Nicolette."

I swallow hard, so overcome with emotion I can't speak for a few moments. "We now know that someone's tried to pose as Nicolette, likely attempting to get information from you."

"They kept asking where I was."

"Of course they did," he says under his breath. "God. So we need to get you with Fabien and Nicolette as soon as possible. The Chaberts want you out of hiding, Savannah. They want you to show your face so they can kill you."

I nod, processing all of it. "So I draw them out," I say. "I let them think I'm not aware it isn't Nicolette. I tell them to meet me somewhere, then we see who we're really dealing with."

Lyam shakes his head. "Too risky."

"No," I insist. "It's the only way, Lyam. I need to testify against them and free Thayer. But I also need to make sure Nicolette is safe, and ultimately that I am, too."

Lyam nods. "Thayer would fucking kill me, but I think it might be our only choice in this case."

I take out my phone and send a text to Nicolette's number.

Me:

> Hey, it's me. I'm guessing you couldn't call, no worries! I miss you so much. It's been a scary time. Where are you?

Nicolette:

> I'm in Paris. Where are you?

Me:

> Paris!!

Nicolette:

> Oh perfect. I want to see you!

My heart thrums at what might happen next.

I look up at Lyam. "She wants to meet. How many are there?"

Mario speaks up. "Only two. That's the good news. Their captain didn't take too kindly to them murdering an officer without permission. It put their entire posse in a compromising position. So there are only two—the two you saw the night of the murder—at large. The bad news? They're pissed off enough they're ready to kill on sight."

Oh, isn't that lovely.

"How'd you find that out?"

Mario smiles in a way that makes my skin prickle. "We have eyes and ears everywhere."

I swallow. "Okay."

Nicolette:

> Let's meet at the Louvre at noon

I read it out loud to Lyam.

"Keep control of the situation," Lyam warns.

I swallow and shake my head before I text back.

Me:

> It's too busy there. Let's meet at Le Square Du Vert-Galant.

Nicolette:

> I'll be there

The triangular public park, near Notre-Dame and the Louvre, is one of my favorite haunts. Raised in tribute to Henry IV, the beautiful square is situated smack dab in the center of the capital. It's not uncommon to see people taking romantic strolls or having picnics, or for couples to take little boat trips for views of the Seine.

Lyam's men can easily hide themselves behind the flowering bushes and majestic trees. And I, for one, will have to be regrettably late for meeting up with my sister.

We go over the plan again, and again, and again.

"And when this is over," Lyam says in a tone that he likely thinks is threatening, "you'll come back here with Thayer, where you belong."

"Oh no I won't," I insist. "I'll go where I think I need to, and I'm not sure where that is yet."

Lyam grits his teeth. "I've never seen my brother so invested in someone so much in my life."

"I don't want him *invested* in me," I snap. "I want him to love me." I swallow the lump in my throat. "Like I love him. And if he thinks the only way to keep me—"

"I already told you why he tracked you," Lyam begins, but I shake my head at him. I have no interest in arguing this point.

I had no idea I was being tracked. I didn't know literally everything I touched was some kind of way to keep me connected to him.

"Question," I say to Lyam. "Before we continue any of this."

"Yes?"

"Can I speak with my sister?"

Lyam clenches his jaw and nods. "Of course." He taps his phone and orders, "Call Fabien."

I want to cry in relief when I hear Fabien's voice on the other end of the line as Lyam joins me to the call. I didn't know how tightly wound I was. I didn't know how emotional I'd be just hearing his voice.

Lyam fills Fabien in. "Can you put Nicolette on the line?"

A few seconds later, I hear her voice.

"Nicolette," I cry into the phone. "Oh, I'm so happy to hear your voice."

I tell her everything and finish up with getting the imposter texts from her. Fabien growls.

"Her phone was destroyed by accident. Someone else sent those texts."

"We've figured that out by now." I frown. "I wonder, if we tapped her number, would we be able to trace them?"

"Possibly," Fabien says. "Lyam's the one to ask. Where are you going now?"

I tell him.

"Lyam, what the hell?" she spits out. "That isn't safe. She doesn't have enough people... My God, Thayer will *kill* you!"

"She'll be safe," Fabien interrupts. "If we leave now. Savannah..." He pauses. "We're on our way."

He hangs up the phone. Lyam stares at me on the screen.

"Savannah. I want you to tell me who you saw kill Officer Leguerre. Be specific, I'm recording."

I tell him everything I remember, the way they looked, our location, the description of the woman they had with them.

"Did you see Thayer kill Officer Leguerre?"

"Of course not. He was with his mother at their family home in Paris."

Lyam nods. "Thank you." He flicks a button on his phone. "This is going to our lawyer and a friend we have on the inside. Thayer's on his way out, thanks to you."

I nod, feeling strangely relieved and apprehensive at the same time. I wanted him out. I want to be safe. But where does that leave us?

TWENTY-ONE

THAYER

"YOUR BROTHER POSTED BAIL."

"Which one?"

I haven't spoken a word since I got here, and at the sound of my voice the other inmates take a step back.

"Lyam."

I think I might hear some take in a quick breath. Sometimes, it's good when a reputation precedes you.

I knew my brothers would be on it. We have connections in Paris, and there's no fucking way I'd stay here long.

Fabien was already in Paris and Lyam at Le Luxe.

"What the fuck are you doing here?" I ask him, blinking in the bright light of day. Jesus, I forgot how miserable it was being locked up.

"Nice to see you, too," he says with a smirk. "I'll tell you everything in the car."

"Where's Savannah? Did you find her?"

Lyam's jaw tightens. "Yeah, we have her."

"Lyam..."

He throws me the keys to the car. "When you get in and I tell you everything, you'll want to be the one driving. Jesus, this isn't like you to be so impatient, and risk being overheard."

"Can you blame me? The woman I love was missing, and I want to make sure she's alright."

"Remember that" is all he says until the car door slams. "Head to Le Square Du Vert-Galant."

By the time he finishes the story, I've got the gas pedal flat to the car floor as houses whizz by. I take the damn corner on two wheels.

"Of all the goddamn—"

"Just go," Lyam says. "You can kill me and Fabien later."

"Oh, I will."

As I drive, Lyam pulls out his phone and hits play. "This has been sent to the chief of police and all lawyers involved in this case. It goes live online in thirty minutes."

He hits play on his phone. I stare at Savannah, telling her side of the story, and clench my fist. I want to reach through the screen and hold her to me. Shield her.

"Who saw that?"

"So far? Me and Fabien. Soon? Everyone."

"If they fucking see that—"

"They won't. They'll be gone by then. This clears your name as well."

I will the car to go even faster.

Lyam's phone rings. Fabien.

"Where are you? Jesus, where *are* you?"

"What's the matter?"

"They called in reinforcements. Must've called in a fucking favor. They think Savannah's here to see her sister, so Nicolette and I are hidden, and we haven't brought enough backup with us. We're outnumbered, Lyam. There's got to be twenty of them ready to take her. They're assembling now."

I drive so fast the needle's buried on the speedometer. I can see the park in front of us.

"What do you have for weapons?"

"Fucking arsenal in the trunk, brother. You have to clear for civilians, Thayer."

"I won't hit civilians."

I never, ever miss.

Then I see her.

Savannah.

She sits on a park bench as pretty as a flower in bloom, placid and calm, a book in her lap. I don't know where Fabien and Nicolette are hidden, but I know they see us. I want to claw myself out of my own skin at the sight of the woman I love in broad daylight, an exposed target without protection. An electric pulse surges through me, propelling me forward. I'll lay down anything and everything to save her.

I bring the car to a stop behind a stone monument, leap out, and arm myself. Lyam follows suit. Everything seems as if we're frozen in time, in slow motion. I need to get to Savannah.

As a man in a suit carrying a briefcase walks by, Lyam grabs his arm.

"What the hell?"

"You walk into that crowd and yell. Say whatever it is you need to. Gun, fire, whatever. You get that crowd the fuck out of that garden, you hear me?"

He stares at the wad of cash Lyam hands him. "Take it and clear these fucking civilians out of here or innocent lives will be lost."

We stand back. He does what we tell him, and seconds later, people run past us.

Savannah looks over at me. Our eyes meet across the lot. I want to kiss her and shake her. I want to fuck her and make her know without a shadow of a doubt she belongs to me. I want to hold her, safe in the crook of my arm, where no one can touch her.

But first, I want to make sure she's safe.

I stalk into the garden with Lyam beside me. Aware of the eyes of our enemies on us, I walk straight to Savannah.

"Fall back," I command in a tone that brooks no argument.

"*Le Sauvage,*" I hear one of them say in a choked voice. Good. I want the memory of every shred of violence I've ever committed replaying in their minds. I want them to imagine their own faces on the bodies of my dead enemies.

Savannah leaps to her feet, an array of emotions written across her face.

"Thayer."

The book on her lap falls to the ground, the pages fluttering like a bird's wings.

I don't care who's here. I don't care about their reinforcements. An army won't keep me from her.

"Come out," I say loud and clear while I hold her eyes. "All of you. You know who I am. You know what I've done. And you know what I'll do if you touch a goddamn hair on her head."

Anything and everything I fucking have to.

Anything.

"Thayer," she repeats.

I sling my arm around her shoulders and face them. I hear footsteps scurrying in the bushes, hushed voices.

I pull out my gun and hold Savannah against me. I draw my weapon and brandish it. "Let's go. You'll have to get through me to get to her."

"That's one of them," she says, pointing to the two men in the front. They stare at me for long seconds. The one she identified turns tail and runs but I shoot, and I don't miss. I hit his leg and he sprawls on the ground. Fabien materializes and takes him.

It was too easy. Too simple. The threat of our attack when we're outnumbered isn't enough to make them run.

A gunshot rings out and Lyam curses, running after someone who's taken off.

"Did they get him?"

"Nicked his shoulder," Fabien says. "He's fine."

"Where's the other one?"

Savannah shakes her head. "I didn't see him. He didn't come."

"Coward."

Fabien and Lyam return, Fabien with one of the murderers in custody and Lyam bleeding, but it's a shallow wound.

"We'll use this one to take us to his friend," Lyam says through gritted teeth.

"I'm going," Savannah says.

"No fucking way." I don't want her hurt.

"There's no time," she says. "I'll stay safe, Thayer, but if we don't get him now, we'll never have peace."

Returning to the car, Lyam slides into the driver's seat and I get in the back with Savannah. He turns the key.

The world around me erupts in smoke.

TWENTY-TWO

SAVANNAH

We're alive. Am I alive? How are we alive?

Smoke billows around us. Was it a smoke bomb? Meant to distract and not to kill?

"Thayer!"

I feel strong arms around me. I gasp and struggle as a painful prick bites my neck.

I try to push them away. I try to flail my arms, but I'm overpowered. I reach for Thayer, but he's behind a wall of flames and smoke. I fall to my knees as my vision blurs. I open my mouth to scream at the sight of a black hood, but my voice is feeble. With a flash of alarm I remember the test I took earlier, as the hood goes over my head and my world fades to blackness.

WHEN I WAKE, it's impossible to tell what time it is because I'm in a darkened room. I try to sit up, but my head is heavy, and my limbs won't move. I blink, trying to make sense of my surroundings.

"She's awake, Sir."

I look over to see the redheaded woman Thayer interviewed sitting beside a man in a dark mask.

"You did well, pet."

I know that voice. Where do I know that voice from?

"They almost escaped, but with your help, they didn't."

"Thank you, Sir. I've learned my lesson and I do my best," she says quietly, her hands folded in her lap. "You've asked that I follow your instructions without question."

I've heard this before. I've heard *them* before, but it's hard to know where or when because my head is so fuzzy.

"Good. Very good."

My wrists are anchored in front of me in an awkward position.

Someone prowls in front of me and shines a light at me. "Put the lights on."

"Yes, Sir."

Dim lights flood the room.

"She is awake," the man says. "You did so well, pet."

The redhead beams and sits beside me. "Do you know why you're here?"

I try to open my swollen lips. "I can guess."

"Why?"

I sigh. "Because I'm the only witness and he doesn't want to go to jail."

The redhead gives me a grim smile and takes out a long, slender knife. She presses it to my neck. "The officer you saw Thayer Gerard murder. You witnessed it firsthand. That night, you were in Paris and neither of you have an alibi. You'll destroy the statement you made and make another."

My head swims. I try to shake it. I didn't see Thayer kill anyone...

"We're giving you a choice, Savannah. We could've killed you very easily."

"You were only pretending to audition for a job," I say through puffy lips.

She shrugs. "Someone had to get in there."

Behind her, her master crosses his arms. "Press harder."

The knife scrapes my skin. I hiss in a breath at the sting.

"You saw him murder that officer, didn't you?"

I grit my teeth. I have to stay alive. This isn't just about me anymore. But if they have me on record testifying against him—*God*. They could make me betray the only man I've ever loved.

She leans in. "We know who you are. We know your sister obtained millions from the Gerard family for being a whore." My pulse spikes. I shake my head. "We know that everything you own is because of her slutty choices. We know that after your parents died, she abandoned you, then tried to make it up with her blood money."

I shake my head. Tears blur my vision as I turn away but turning away only makes her press the knife harder. I stifle a cry as I feel my skin tear.

"We know what you saw. And this is a warning, Savannah. You will testify against Thayer in court. If you don't do what we say, we promise, no one you know will be safe. Not Nicolette, or her husband, and least of all Thayer."

I shake my head. "He didn't do it."

I don't know what they'll do to me, but I can't let them hurt me.

"He did, though, and you saw it because you were with him. You were both in Paris the night of the murder. You saw him murder that officer, didn't you?"

When I don't respond, the man growls at her. "Cut her."

Her eyes, wide and terrified, plead for forgiveness as she obeys him. I scream out loud as the knife cuts me. I'm trying to move away from the knife when I have an idea.

I sit up and turn to her. "No!" I scream. "I won't!"

"Hurt her!"

With a cry, she slices at me with the knife. I yank out of her way just in time and throw my hands in front of my face. The knife slices through rope, nicking me but freeing my hands.

The door to the room bursts open. I see Thayer in a pool of light, his weapons drawn.

"Thayer!"

"One down," he says placidly, a look of tranquility on his face as he points his gun at the man. "One to go."

The man's eyes go wide as he puts his hands up. Thayer doesn't shoot to kill, though. With a look of pure malice, he shoots the man's kneecap and makes him fall to the floor.

The woman screams and lunges for Thayer, but I grab her by the hair and yank her back. She falls to the floor. I kneel on her back and keep her down. I push the same knife she used on me against her neck.

"Go ahead. Try me."

Thayer yells over his shoulder, "Get her out of here for questioning."

Lyam enters and takes the redhead bodily out of the room. "Naughty girl," he chides, clearly enjoying himself. "You're in big, big trouble for this."

Thayer grabs the man by the neck.

"Apologize to her."

The man glares at me. Thayer grits his teeth and backhands him so hard he falls to the floor and screams.

"I said, apologize," he repeats as he makes the man face me again.

"I'm sorry," the man says. My stomach turns at the sight of his teeth, reddened with blood.

"Good. Savannah, you have a choice," Thayer says to me. "You can step outside with Fabien and Nicolette. They're waiting for you. Or you can stay here with me while I get rid of the last threat against you."

The man's eyes go wide, and he begins to shake.

Back in the alley, which seems so long ago now, I saw the look of terror on his captive's face. He would have killed me and forced Thayer to serve time for a murder he didn't commit.

I cross my arms over my chest. I'm not leaving Thayer's side again.

Not ever again.

"I'll stay."

TWENTY-THREE

S*AVANNAH*

I COULD HAVE LEFT. I could have chosen ignorance. I could have decided to turn a blind eye.

But I couldn't.

I love Thayer, and that means loving every facet of him – even the unapologetically violent part of him that lives by a moral code so foreign to me it's almost written in a foreign language.

I had to witness him see this through.

I had to watch him take the life of the man who would have tortured and killed me.

Loving him doesn't mean turning my back on who he is, but accepting *all* of him.

I don't know if I'll ever be able to erase the image of what I heard and saw tonight. His cold, calculated voice and vicious, merciless actions.

I don't know if I want to.

I've made the decision to stay. I've made the decision to love him.

And that means, I've made the decision to accept the code he lives by. I don't want to shield my eyes from the fierce, sometimes cruel, reality of who he is.

If I love him, then I love all of him.

When we're done – when my wounds are doctored and he calls in his cleanup crew to dispose of the last vestiges of violent and certain justice –

We go home.

Back to the Gerard family home.

When we arrive, bloodied and bruised, our clothing torn and ragged, his mother doesn't even blink. "I'll put you in the guest suite on the second floor," she says pragmatically. "Do you need a doctor?"

Her inkling that we're a couple might have something to do with the fact that he's carrying me, and my arms are strewn around his neck.

Thayer shakes his head. "We've seen a doctor already. Everything else we need is in the suite."

Not surprisingly, Thayer growled and cursed at the knife wound, insisting I get it cleaned up and bandaged.

I wonder what he has in that suite...

She nods. "Are you officially here?" Avril Gerard asks Thayer tentatively.

He gives her a wry smile. "I didn't escape jail. I was released. I won't be going back. So yes, I'm officially here and you don't have to cover for me."

She breathes out a sigh of relief and looks at me. "You two are together?"

I entwine my fingers with his and swallow hard.

A fierce realization hits me. I shouldn't have left. I see now that I let my fear dictate my choices. Nothing, no person or danger or power on this earth, will keep me away from him.

I saw the way he looked at me. I saw the look in his eyes when he came for me. And I know why.

I know that Thayer loves me, and I know I'll never, ever settle for anything less than this fierce, consuming, intense love of his. Of ours.

"We are."

Avril smiles, her whole pretty face lighting up. "Good," she says simply. "I'm happy to hear that."

We head upstairs. The events of the past few days weigh heavily on my mind. I play them over and over and over again, until I wish I could push *pause* on the replay button and stop for a little while. I don't want to think about any of this anymore.

Thayer and I have hardly said two words to each other.

And now it's time.

I've been here many times, but I've really only ever seen the majestic, beautiful rooms they use for entertaining. I've never seen the inside of any of the bedrooms, much less his.

When I came here seeking refuge, I never imagined I'd be where I am today.

With Thayer... as his.

In his bedroom.

Craving a reconnection that transcends words, discussion, dialogue, and anything that human frailty demands to clumsily find our way back to truth and togetherness. Craving a reconnection that only the two of us understand.

On the cusp of telling him news that will change our lives forever.

We kiss on the landing. At first, it's sweet and poignant. My cheeks are wet with tears at the feel of his fingers in my hair, his lips on mine, and the naked truth of who we are together. As we kiss, my protests fall away like our disguises, leaving nothing but our true selves. I can hardly remember why I turned away to begin with.

With every step he takes toward his room, toward being alone and bared to each other once more, our kiss grows more sensual. The thrilling touch of his tongue to mine. The tingling current of arousal that threads its way through my belly and between my legs. The swelling of my breasts pressed up against the wall of his chest. The ache to be filled by him.

The door shuts behind us like an afterthought.

He slides me down the length of his body to the floor so he can stand me up, then holds me as he drops to his knees, kissing his way down the length of my body. I gasp when he kisses my belly.

Does he know?

"Thayer," I whisper, threading my fingers through his hair as he moans against my skin, as if savoring the scent, taste, and feel of me, committing them to memory.

"Savannah." His voice is choked, vibrating with emotion. He's as vulnerable as a child when he meets my eyes, every guard he's ever put up gone and in its place nothing but love and adoration. "I thought I lost you. I thought they won. I made the decision that I would find you, that I would fight for you, that I'd do whatever it took to find you again and bring you back to me."

Kneeling in front of me, he presses his face to my thighs and wraps his arms around me, embracing me. Holding me to him as if he never wants to let me go.

"Thayer," I repeat, my own voice tremulous. "I knew. I knew deep down inside that you'd come for me. I left because I was so angry with you. But I know now why you did what you did."

"Yes," he says, his voice taking on the harsh tone I'm so familiar with. "And I'd do it again. Jesus, woman, are you in a world of trouble when I get you back to the club."

I can't help but smile at that. I'm here for it.

"We're going to put this all behind us," he says. He saw to it with his own hands that no one will come after me now. Finally, *finally,* the danger has passed and now we face... us.

"I have something to tell you."

His gaze meets mine and I can't hold it in any longer.

"I'm pregnant," I blurt out. After everything we've been through, he needs to know.

He blinks. Looks up at me as if I'd just told him I decided to move to outer space. Cups my ass in his big, strong hands and stares up at me.

"Say that again."

Okay, so it's safe to say he *didn't* know.

I swallow the lump in my throat but can't stop my voice from coming out all trembly. "I'm pregnant," I repeat, this time on a whisper.

"You're pregnant," he repeats. "And you *left*?"

Uh oh. Now this is the Thayer I know.

Then he's on his feet and I'm in his arms and he's stalking to the big bed nestled in the corner of the room. It's immaculate in here, as if no one's been here in ages. I smile to myself at the obvious sign of Thayer's perfectionism. Not a pillow out of place, as tidy as could be.

"They're lucky they're dead," he growls. "They're fucking lucky they're gone. If I'd known—my God, I wish I could kill them all over again."

Only Thayer.

I cup his jaw in my hand and bring his eyes to mine. "No more killing tonight, okay? No more ending dangerous threats or pounding your chest or brandishing weapons," I plead with him. "Make love to me, Thayer."

And so he does. In silence, we strip each other's clothes off and toss them away, the remnants of a battle we fought and won.

We make our way to the bathroom hand in hand and shower together.

We lather each other up and wash every trace of violence from our bodies.

He kneels in front of me and worships my breasts, my thighs, my pussy. He licks and fingers and gropes me until I'm half out of my mind. I convince him to stand under the steaming hot water while I get on *my* knees and take his cock in my mouth. I relish the feel of his hands in my wet hair, his powerful thighs beneath my palms, the way he moans when I lick and suckle. He pulls out before he comes and yanks me to my feet.

Pressed up against the wall, he spreads my legs apart and lines his cock up at my entrance. I brace myself on the tile and moan at the first feel of his savage thrust. My sex clenches around him. The lump in my throat dissolves, and the tears wash away in the steady stream of water.

"You're mine, Savannah." I throw my head back as he thrusts again. "I love you."

A thrill passes through me. "And I love you," I whisper.

We make love, in this savage way of ours. He's a savage but he's *my* savage and I wouldn't have him any other way.

I'm overpowered by him as I surrender, and nothing's ever felt so right.

"I love you," he repeats. "And I'm asking that you let me love you the only way I know how."

Is this Thayer, my badass savage, asking me for permission?

I sniff and nod. "Of course," I say as he stills within me, his cock and my sex throbbing. "I would love that."

"Not always."

"Maybe not always," I concede with a laugh.

"And if you ever leave me again," he says with a powerful thrust that feels both punishing and scalding, "you will see all that Le Luxe has to offer in the way of punishment."

I smile and shiver. I don't want him to punish me, and I don't ever plan on leaving, but I am totally here for finding out all that Le Luxe has to offer.

We lapse into silence as we chase our pleasure. I peak when he does, his moans of pleasure mingling with mine. My body's numb with pleasure and my knees tremble. He holds me against him as the hot water pelts against my heated skin.

"Thayer," I whisper. "I'm sorry." I turn to face him and bury my face in his neck. His arms come around me and he holds me, our naked skin pressed up against each other, steam rising like hope, engulfing us. "I shouldn't have left. I should've trusted you."

"I hate that you left, but not for the reasons you think. I hate that you left because I wanted you to trust me, and I didn't even trust you enough to tell you I tracked you. I did it behind your back, and there's no excuse for that."

I let myself feel the warmth of my head against his shoulder. The comfort of his arms around me. The safety of being cocooned against him with the knowledge that our enemies are no longer a threat, we no longer have to hide, and we both know where we stand.

"We could stay here for a long time apologizing and reliving things," I say finally. "How about you take me back to your bed and show me how you make love to a pregnant woman?"

FABIEN AND NICOLETTE sit in the living room of the Gerard family residence in Paris. Lyam sits in front of the fire scowling at a length of rope in his hand, trying to fashion a knot or something similar.

Fabien eyes us warily, Nicolette squeezes my hand, and Avril flits to and fro bringing hot tea, a platter of her kitchen's pastries, a decadent cheese board, and wine gifted to them from the Rossi family.

At the sight of the wine, Thayer whisks it away and shakes his head with a muted, "She can't have that," to his mother.

I stifle a giggle.

Nicolette's eyes widen.

"Savannah," she asks slowly. "Is there a *reason* you won't drink the Rossi wine? It's your favorite."

"She's pregnant," Thayer blurts out, causing his mother to gasp, Nicolette's jaw to drop open, and Fabien to chuckle in that Gerard-brother dark way.

"Jesus," Lyam says. "That didn't take you long."

Avril grins. "I've always said when Thayer fell, he'd fall hard. I *knew* it. I just knew it, from that very first day you two were arguing in the foyer and you asked me to tell him to be nice to you."

"Did you?" I ask, sipping my very non-alcoholic cup of tea.

"I did," she beams. "It's not his way to casually date or to think a long time about the right decisions. When Thayer knows what he wants, he is all in, and with you, my love, he is *all in*. A baby!" She embraces me so tightly I can hardly breathe, and I hug her back.

God, it feels good to have a mother again.

"Hormones," I say, as I swipe at the stubborn tears on my cheeks that *will* continue no matter what. Everything makes me cry these days. "I cry over everything."

"It's okay," Nicolette says warmly, her own eyes shimmering. "I guess it's time for me to admit my baby sister's growing up."

"*Grown* up," Thayer growls, as if the implication he's robbed the cradle's too much for him to handle. "Grown. Up."

"Grown up," Nicolette agrees. "Oh, Savannah."

"Before we get all mushy," Lyam says, ever the pragmatist, "We need to make sure we've closed the door on every threat against us and communicate every detail."

He looks to his mother. "Your choice if you stay or go."

She looks around the small group of us with nothing short of adoration in her gaze. "I'll go," she says softly. "Savannah?"

I hold Thayer's hand. "I'll stay for now but join you shortly. Didn't you say something about a gâteau?"

"I did." She looks at me warmly, her eyes shining. "You name it, and I'll make sure you and the baby have it."

"We won't be having any spoiled children," Thayer says grumpily.

"You say that now," Fabien mutters.

Avril leaves, chuckling to herself, and as soon as the door shuts behind her, Lyam speaks up. "I want to give a full report on what I've found before we close this door." We all sit up straighter. I'm sure the brothers are mostly concerned with the Chabert family's antics, but I want to know what Cosette had to do with this.

"I take full responsibility," he begins. "I was the one that brought the women in for hire. And yes, Mindy was a member of Le Luxe, but I had no idea she had any affiliation with the Chaberts and that her master was on their payroll. To be fair, they hid it well, and have attended Le Luxe for years, but it's a good indication we need more thorough background checks."

"Absolutely." Thayer scowls in agreement. "And Cosette?"

For a second, it looks like Thayer and Lyam are going to get into a fight. Lyam's eyes flash and Thayer sits up straighter. I look at Nicolette in a panic, but she watches them placidly as she sips her wine. She's seen their bluster before.

"Cosette was threatened," Lyam says. "She's riddled with guilt over everything."

"What did they threaten her with?" Fabien asks, and I wonder if I've imagined that smug look on his face.

Lyam scowls. "They were going to kill me."

No one speaks for a few moments. Lyam clears his throat. "Cosette has submitted her resignation." He looks to Thayer. "The final call is yours."

"If she's tendered her resignation, then the decision is hers." Thayer looks to me. "And what are your thoughts, Savannah? You were the one she threatened."

I swallow hard and think about it before I answer. "I think Cosette has always been trustworthy. She's loyal and a good friend to Nicolette. She acted under duress, and I hate to think that Lyam or she would've been hurt if she hadn't complied." I blow out a breath. "It's tricky. I don't blame her for wanting to leave, but at the same time, I would think, given how things played out, you won't find anyone more loyal going forward. What kind of message does that send your enemies? They've weakened your family with their bullshit? No. I think you should send the message they've been unable to break you."

Nicolette nods. "I agree."

Fabien nods. "Well played, Savannah. I'm impressed."

A small but clear indication they don't see me as a child.

I smile. I'll take it.

Lyam blows out a breath. "I promise you. I'll keep a very close eye on her."

Thayer scowls. "I'll hold you to that."

I shiver and lean in a little closer to Thayer. I'm not sure he'll ever soften, and I'm not sure I'll ever want him to.

As if reading my mind, Thayer places his hand on my knee and gives me a gentle squeeze. My heart swells.

I once feared what Thayer was capable of. I once feared what he'd done. But now, I love who he is. I love knowing that he will protect me no matter the cost, and that our family—our small, growing family—will always be dear to him.

He loves me, and I know with certainty...

I.

Love.

Him.

EPILOGUE

Savannah

PARIS.

Is.

Awesome ... with Thayer.

God, I thought I loved Paris *before,* when I could roam the city streets and peruse the bookstores, drink a café au lait with a hot, freshly baked croissant while devouring my latest favorite book. When I could stroll through the art museums and galleries and tour the Louvre, or sit on a park bench and immerse myself in the city and culture and the lilting beauty of the language.

Turns out, it's even better when I don't do it all alone, or tag along as the third wheel with my sister and Fabien.

Let me be clear. In no way, shape, or form has Thayer loosened up. If anything, he's *more* protective to the point of damn near stifling now that I'm carrying his baby, but now...I like it.

It's cute how he lifts my mug of steaming hot coffee and blows on it before he hands it to me. The way he sits beside me on the bench and whispers sweet nothings in his native tongue, massages my back in bed where I lay to quell the nausea while reading a book.

The way he rests his hand on my gently swollen abdomen and tells the baby how much he or she is loved.

He has no interest or patience in the art museums but hey, a girl can't have everything.

Now that my days are filled with companionship and family, my nights with endless lovemaking in the passionate arms of a French lover, I find the words for my romance novel are *flying*. Who knew this was my genre?

He knows I love Paris, so we visit frequently. The trip from Paris to Corsica's easy with a private jet, really no different than a quick business excursion.

And holy *hell,* does he make good on his promise to show me what Le Luxe has to offer.

It's almost a bit unnerving how easily the danger against us fades. It's definitely a bit shocking how many people the Gerard brothers have working for them, including a large group of police officers they know well who are absolutely in their pockets and more than happy to compensate them for punishing the man that killed their fellow officer.

The Gerard men, most especially Thayer, are fastidious and hardworking, and incredibly efficient at what they do, which is a whole lot of things I want to know nothing about. Nicolette has promised me that it's much better not knowing the finer intricacies of their business, and there are times when I totally agree with her. This is one of those times.

When I'm carrying his baby, content in the knowledge that he loves me above all others. That the life that stretches before me is no longer as lonely as I once feared it would be. Not with him by my side.

"What do you think," Thayer says thoughtfully, playing with my hair in an absentminded way that I find incredibly endearing, "about finishing your degree? You have a few more classes to take, and it would be a shame for you not to follow through."

"You'd let me go to a big, large university, teeming with people, apart from you?" I tease.

He visibly winces and his eyebrows draw together. "Well, let's not get carried away."

I laugh out loud. "Then what did you have in mind?"

"Something... local. Or maybe...online or something?"

I give him a smile and shake my head. "I think that's an excellent idea. I love that idea. I can actually finish my degree in a few months."

"Perfect."

"Why does that matter to you?" I ask him curiously.

He gives me that signature scowl, the one that makes him look daring and reckless, like he should be a swashbuckling pirate. "Because it matters to *you*."

Oh. Well, that should've been clear enough.

"So you're not one of those old-fashioned mobsters who thinks his wife is a pretty little trophy to keep on a shelf until he tires of her and decides he needs a younger, newer model? I hear mistresses are quite common..."

Thayer's dark eyes flash at me with a wicked smile that makes me yelp.

"I think you know me well enough by now to know I am absolutely old-fashioned and painfully loyal."

"Which means..."

He leans in and kisses my cheek while he whispers in my ear, "That I will be devoted to you until the day I die."

My heart squeezes. I never knew I wanted — no *needed* — someone so fiercely protective ... until Thayer.

I know it matters to him that I'm safe. That I'm cared for. That I'm loved.

"Maman called," he says as I stretch my arms over my head and he gives me a little tickle. I squeal and lean closer into him, so he embraces me and holds me against him.

"And?"

"She wanted to know if we'd visit for dinner soon."

I smile. "I would *love* that." We sit together and enjoy amicable silence in the quiet, warm evening. When a surprisingly brisk wind kicks up, he wordlessly wraps his arm around me and shields me from the cold. I wonder if it isn't maybe a bit symbolic — he may not ever be able to protect me from everything, but maybe it's alright that he shields me a little. Maybe there's a part of both of us that needs something exactly like this, this mutual meeting of each other's needs.

"And what about the threats against us?"

"Us," he says with a rare smile. "God, I love hearing you say that." He blows out a breath. "To answer your question, there probably will always be forces against us, Savannah. The key to it all, I've learned, is to stay close together. It's so much harder for anyone to harm us knowing we're a fortress."

Fortress. I like that.

"Right. Well that makes sense."

I think about Nicolette and Fabien, and whatever it is that brought her to him. She may never tell me all the details, and I'm okay with that.

I think about Lyam and Cosette, and how closely she escaped with her life. I know typically that betrayal the likes of hers warrants swift and severe punishment. But I can still see her pinched face and pale cheeks as she pleaded with me for forgiveness for a sin against me I didn't know she'd committed.

I know that this life I've chosen is complex and beautiful and heartbreaking...and I wouldn't have it any other way.

"Let's go home," he says softly, threading his fingers through mine.

I smile. We rise, hand in hand.

And walk home.

PREVIEW

POSSESS ME

Book 3 of "Masters of Corsica"

Chapter 1

Lyam

Boom.

A thrill goes through me when I pull the trigger. *Always.*

If I believed in super powers, I'd know what mine is: I hit with the first shot.

Fuck flying or seeing through walls. Give me a cold, hard weapon, ammunition, and a target.

Sometimes I feel like my body's connected to my gun, as if it's a part of my actual being. An extension of my person. When I shoot, my mind and body fuse.

There's something almost divine about watching your bullet hit the target. There's nothing methodical or rote about it. Pulling the trigger and hitting a target's makes me feel godlike. I have the power, right in the palm of my hand, to end life.

You don't know how heavy a body is until you watch it collapse. You don't know how red blood is until you see it spill. You don't know the power you wield until you look into the eyes of another person whose life you're about to end.

Boom.

I've got a variety of places I like to go for target practice but today, I wanted to shatter glass. So I came to one of my favorite spots in Paris: a private, remote field we've bought for this purpose. Traditional practice inside for when it's cold or snowing, but my favorite — a brick wall where I line up glass bottles. My friends who know my favorite hobby save empty bottles and give them to me by the bucket.

I love watching the glass explode. I love the *boom* of the gunshot. The sharp crack of shattering glass, followed by a rainstorm of tiny, brilliant sparking shards.

I pull the trigger again and the cobalt blue bottle on the far right disintegrates.

"Jesus."

My bodyguard, Philippe, shakes his head. "How far away is that target?"

I squint at it and shrug. "A hundred meters."

"Mon dieu."

Some shooters routinely shoot fifty yards, but hunters and sharpshooters can easily hit targets at further distances, depending on the weapon. I like to practice long range. I don't always have my target bound, on their knees in front of me, served up on a silver platter.

I aim for the next blue bottle and smile at the memory of Thayer handing me a case of empties after his honeymoon, when my phone rings.

God, I fucking hate technology. Obtrusive and obnoxious, a man can't even take a piss in private without some kinda goddamn interference.

Speak of the devil. It's Thayer.

"Yeah?"

"She's ready for you."

A different kind of thrill runs through me. I know exactly who he's talking about.

There was a time when I would have moved heaven and earth to be alone with Cosette, but she ruined that. She's earned the ultimate penalty for betraying my family: execution.

But Cosette is too beautiful to die.

My brothers agreed to allow her to live, but she'll suffer the consequences. Namely, she'll answer to me.

My job is to keep her in my custody. Punish her betraying my family.

I stand and slide my gun, the metal still hot to the touch, into a harness at my waist. I don't go anywhere without a weapon, which has made for some strategic planning.

I roll my neck and stretch my shoulders.

My plane is ready for me. Cosette's been kept prisoner at Le Luxe, the master slave sex club owned by Thayer. But I've already made my decision.

I won't keep her there, where she has friends and acquaintances. I won't keep her anywhere near easy access to an escape. I've already made my decision.

I'll bring her back to Paris.

Here, I can make sure that she'll never betray us again. Here, I can keep a closer eye on her.

And here, I'm closest to the people I need to destroy.

"Hey, man." Philippe grins at me and shows me a bag of shots. He mouths, "You want a nip on the plane?"

I grin back and move my mouth away from the mouthpiece. "You fucking know it."

Thayer doesn't need to know. My older brother's the most serious asshole I know, would kick Philippe's ass for drinking on the job. He'd roll his eyes at me and talk about the loss of control, the need for precision and focus, but I don't fucking care. Sometimes, it takes the edge off.

I grab one and slide it into my pocket. I'll drink it on the plane.

"For one goddamn time I wish you'd take a ride," Thayer says. "Do you have any idea how much easier that would be for us?"

I clench my jaw. "No."

I don't get rides places. I drive my own cars and I like it that way.

"For Christ's, Lyam. You should really consider trusting the people we hire. You know we vet the fuck out of them."

"No."

Why does he have to harp on about this?

He blows out an angry breath on the other side of the line.

"Lyam, you should reconsider."

"Why?" I ask, as I slide into the driver's seat and start the engine. "You know I prefer driving my own car."

He curses. "Because people know you're someone important. They respect you. Because if anything happened, you could shoot instead of having to navigate a fucking car."

I shake my head. "I don't need a driver to get respect." Shooting once and being a trained assassin will do that just fine. And if that fails to work, I have other methods of earning respect. "And I can handle myself."

I transfer the call to the car speakers.

He drops the subject. "Fine, suit yourself."

"I will. After I park, I want you to get one of my men to take the car back." I take a turn left when Philippe shakes his head.

"What?"

"That won't be necessary, sir."

"What the fuck are you talking about?"

"I was going to tell you about that—"

It's not often that Thayer sounds apologetic, and it gets my fucking hackles up.

My voice is low and controlled when I respond. "Tell me about *what*?"

Up ahead I see a flash of black. I narrow my eyes at the signature uniform of the *gendarmerie* and slow down to get a better look.

Two of them, unfamiliar to me. One man has a tattoo on lower right arm, until recently, forbidden. The other's a woman with short black hair.

I draw in a breath and let it go.

I don't know them. They're not my targets.

They weren't there.

In my mind's eye I see a flash of rope, hear the clink of chains, and the insidious laughter of the uniformed men. It takes me a minute to realize that Thayer was still talking.

"...and I thought it better that she be brought here instead."

"Who brought her?"

He pauses before he snaps, "Did you hear a fucking word I said?"

"Of course I did," I lie, as I take the turn down the main road that takes me to my family home in Paris, the same road that was supposed to take me to the airport.

"I said, I had Claude bring her back."

"How?" I snap.

"How? What the fuck are you talking about?"

Beside me, Philippe stiffens. My voice is low and unamused when I ask, "Did he touch her?"

"Of course he didn't touch her. He knows better than to take advantage of her. Lyam, who do you think we hired?"

"No," I say, my jaw clenched. "I meant did he put a hand on her in any way, shape, or form? Did he hold her arm? Grab her if she stumbled?" My hand begins to ache and I realize I'm holding the phone too tight. "She's mine, Thayer. We agreed. I don't want anyone else to even look at her."

I can hear Thayer swallowing on the other end of the line. "Fuck. I don't know the answer to that. I'm sorry, Lyam. I should've sent you."

Philippe squirms on his seat. I ignore him.

Thayer continues. "Fabien said that you wanted her in Paris, so he had her sent to Paris. He thought it would be the most expedient."

"Expedient my ass." I grit my teeth. "We agreed. She's mine. I'm the one that makes sure she never betrays our family again. I'm the one that makes sure she understands the severity of what she did. Me. No one else. Fucking *me*."

"I got you, brother. I get it. Why do you think we let her go? If it were anyone else..."

I know. Woman or no, she'd have died a slow and painful death.

I draw in a breath and let it out slowly.

"I'm almost there."

"Lyam, don't kill him," Thayer says. "Send him back here and I'll make sure you never see him again. He's good people."

I nod. "I'll find out how the trip went and I won't do anything without talking to you first."

Thayer curses. "Alright. Okay, I got it. Listen, Savannah and I will be in Corsica. Keep an eye on Maman?"

"Of course." I have my own residence in Paris, but my mother's only about thirty minutes away. "When do they land?"

"Fabien arranged for a car to take her to you."

I grit my teeth and take in a deep breath so I can fabricate patience.

It doesn't work.

"When. Do. They. Land?"

"Ten minutes."

I hang up the phone before I curse him out.

It's unlike my brothers to keep me in the dark like this. I know the only reason why they did was because they had to choose a more expedient route but I don't like not knowing when the playing field changes.

"Sir, I know Claude. He wouldn't touch her. He would know better."

Maybe so but I don't like the idea. I was only here waiting for one of our private jets to return or I'd already be in Corsica.

When I don't respond, Philippe looks at a window. "There's talk about us publicly today. Did you hear that?"

"Excuse me?"

"Did you hear Montague's recent declaration? Party line? Fabien and Thayer said they're not afraid of him, but..."

"We're not afraid of anybody," I correct, but it's only so he doesn't hear the real concern in my voice. "When did he say this?"

"Last night," he explains. "It was on the news. I saw a clip online."

"Pull it up."

François Montague looms on the screen, larger than life.

Red hot hatred pulses through my veins. I turn away, grip the steering wheel, and focus in front of me when something scratches at my memory.

I know that location...

"Where is he?"

"I'm not sure."

It's familiar....

"Louvre and Tuileries?"

The Louvre and Tuileries district of Paris brushes The Seine in the south, with the neighborhoods known as Bourse and The Grand Boulevards to the north. Ah. He's in front of the green trees that border the Tuileries gardens.

My apartment's only a few blocks away.

Even in my peripheral vision I can see his jowls sag as he talks. I despise the pompous bastard.

He continues in his despicable, oily voice. "As the citizens of Paris have shown great concern regarding the infiltration of organized crime into our historic and precious city, the focus of my campaign to run for reelection focuses primarily on bringing them down. My promise to you, the people of Paris, is to bring them into custody and eradicate their influence and presence. We will bring safety and honesty back to our historical landmark of a city."

"Oh for the love of God," I say with disdain. "Of all the fucking platforms to run. What a fucking asshole."

Philippe snorts. "The irony of it is that the political parties are more corrupt than you are."

"You've got that fucking right."

The camera pans to the left as I cruise to a stop at a light. The sun has begun its descent, the sky darkening.

I blink and stare at the man on the screen. He's familiar. Have I been him before? Why can't I place him? I know in my gut I haven't just seen him on the screen but in person. Where? Why does my skin crawl? Something about him that makes me check my gun to make sure it's loaded.

Other people check to see if they shut off the stove or locked the door.

I check to make sure I have enough ammo.

Normally, I wouldn't give two shits about a politician running his mouth about organized crime. The only ones they ever catch are the ones that are too dumb to hide their actions or too arrogant to try. The new ones. The more established groups like us don't fear the police force because we're smart enough to have half of their goddamn force on our payroll.

This time, though... this time, something doesn't feel quite right.

The light turns green as I drive toward the airport.

"They're waiting, sir."

I exit the car, thankful dusk has fallen so I can stand in the shadows and observe them. I stroke my gun lovingly and wish Princess was with me.

I like my toys and pets.

The door opens.

And then I see her.

Cosette.

Tall and slender and as delicate as a porcelain doll.

I thought I loved her once.

I know now that I was dumb and foolish and there's no such thing as romantic love, and definitely not with someone like Cosette.

Seems she has a similar memory, because when she sees me, she narrows her eyes and juts her chin out as if to defy me before I even command her.

Claude, on the other hand, does *not* see me.

I watch as he doesn't just touch her but fucking *manhandles* her off the plane.

"Let *go*," she seethes. "Don't touch me like that."

She fights and resists him, then for a few seconds I don't see anything but a haze of red.

"Oh, fuck," Philipe curses beside me as I step into the light.

Claude sees me.

I walk faster. I'm only paces away now.

In seconds, his eyes go wide in terror and he does the only thing worse than touching my woman — he pushes her away from him.

She's restrained so can't brace her fall.

On instinct, I catch her, just in time.

I don't bother to ask if she's alright. I don't bother to check her. I plunk her down on the tarmac and cock my gun because Claude just fucking ran.

When I shoot to kill, I don't miss.

I'm not trying to kill him.

Yet.

I shoot and hit the back of his kneecap with the first shot. He falls, screaming, and grabs at his knee. Brilliant red blood stains the ground around him. I shoot his second knee just to fucking hurt him.

When I reach him, I grab him off the ground and lift him to his feet. He screams like a stuck pig.

"Lyam," Cosette shouts at me from the car. "He didn't hurt me, Lyam. I promise he didn't."

She's a sensitive soul who can't stand the sight of violence or blood. Of course she's trying to save his ass.

My voice is low and sinister when I reply, making sure the threat is loud and clear.

"I didn't ask if he hurt you. He's smart enough to know that if he hurt you, he'd wish for death before I killed him."

"Sir, I was only doing what your brother said. I was only—"

"Laying your disgusting hand on *my* hostage? And then after you fucking wet your pants when you saw me, let her go so she nearly fell? Do you have any goddamn sense in your head?"

I don't know why her pleas sway me. I won't kill him, not in front of her.

I lift my gun and snap the butt against his temple. He cries out in pain as I strike him again, and again before I push him toward Philippe.

"Take him back to Corsica."

"But sir — he'll need a medic."

"He can wait on the plane. Back to Corsica, *now*."

I turn my back to them and reach for Cosette.

"And you." I take her hand and yank her to her feet. "Will come with me.

PREORDER HERE (Releases April 14, 2023)

"Possess Me" QR code

What to read next? Check out Jane Henry's bestselling trilogy "Wicked Doms" for $.99 or FREE on Kindle Unlimited

"Wicked Doms Box Set" QR code

Jane Henry

Fueled by dark chocolate and even darker coffee, USA Today bestselling author Jane Henry writes what she loves to read – character-driven, unputdownable romance featuring dominant alpha males and the powerful heroines who bring them to their knees. She's believed in the power of love and romance since Belle won over the beast, and finally decided to write love stories of her own.

[Click here to be notified of Jane's new releases!](#)

Jane's Website

- bookbub.com/profile/jane-henry
- facebook.com/janehenryromance
- instagram.com/janehenryauthor
- amazon.com/Jane-Henry/e/B01BYAQYYK
- tiktok.com/@janehenryauthor

Printed in Great Britain
by Amazon